"GOD, WHY AM I SO AFRAID?"

"God, why am I so afraid?"

By Donovan Marshall
Illustrated by Kathy Counts

Publishing House
St. Louis

Copyright © 1982 Concordia Publishing House
3558 S. Jefferson Avenue, St. Louis, MO 63118

Manufactured in the United States of America

Library of Congress Cataloging in Publication Data

Marshall, Donovan, 1908-
    God, why am I so afraid?

    (God, why series)
    Summary: Thirteen-year-old Dawn's summer in the Colorado mountains with her
father and brother helps her to conquer her fear of almost everything, and leads her and
new friends to prove a theory that an advanced Indian culture once existed in that area.
    [1. Fear—Fiction. 2. Fathers and daughters—Fiction
3. Christian life—Fiction] I. Title. II. Series.
PZ7.M35647Go   [Fic]   82-7360
ISBN 0-570-03630-5 (pbk.)   AACR2

1 2 3 4 5 6 7 8 9 10 PP 91 90 89 88 87 86 85 84 83 82

**To my wife Estelle
who has never failed to lend
her encouragement and inspiration
to my writing efforts**

Chapter One

"I guess a pastor's family wouldn't be afraid of such things as ghosts." The tall boy who brought our groceries over from the village market put the sacks on the kitchen table and stood there grinning at me.

He was just joking, I know, but he didn't know how frightened I was of everything—everything! The idea of spending a whole summer in a strange town, in a cabin out in the woods, with spiders and creeping, crawling things, the pitch-dark nights, heights, and all the other things had sent chills down my spine. Now he was introducing me to still another horror—a ghost. *O God, why am I so afraid of everything?*

The delivery boy's grin faded as if he had overheard my silent prayer. "I wasn't making fun of you," he said. "I mean I wasn't trying to scare you—honest."

I believed him. "I'm like that," I answered. Over the years I'd learned to make fun of myself and my fears partly to cover up the constant shaky feeling in my stomach. "I'm scared of my shadow."

He smiled, and I liked the way his blue eyes had sort of crinkles at the corners. Suddenly I noticed how I must look to him. I'm not a beauty, but my nose is straight, and my brown hair goes pretty well with my gray eyes. But I'd been helping Mom clean the cabin and get things organized in the kitchen, and I looked a mess. My last birthday was my thirteenth, and I guess I'm a little more concerned about how I look. Mom says that's natural.

"It struck me funny because you looked so surprised," he

said, "and I didn't know if it was because of the ghosts or because I knew your father was a minister." He was grinning again. "There aren't many secrets in Gold Mountain."

"How about the secret of the lost gold mine?" asked my brother, who has an annoying habit of appearing out of nowhere and joining in strictly private conversations.

"The lost mine sure isn't a secret—except maybe where to find it and what's in it. Some people aren't even sure it's a mine at all." The delivery boy turned his good-natured grin on Peter. "Everybody looks for it sooner or later."

"Well—but what's the bad rap about our cabin being haunted?" Peter had just turned twelve and joined the Boy Scouts. He seemed to think that gave him a license to be a private detective.

"Forget it!" our visitor told him. "It's just like you say—a bad rap—a campfire story. Guess I was mostly trying to make conversation." The new boy was at least a head taller than Peter. His blond hair had a wind-blown look, but it looked freshly combed compared to my brother's uncombed reddish brush.

"When do we get to the story? Does it have to be around a campfire?" A private eye does not give up easily.

"Tell you what—" The delivery boy paused in the doorway. "I'm off this afternoon. If you want me to, I can show you the town. Bring you up to date on the ghost stuff at the same time." He was looking at me as he spoke.

My brother snorted. "We can see the whole village from here. But we'll take you up on the offer."

I didn't always let my brother get away with speaking for me. He had a way of getting me into situations that weren't too comfortable. This time I didn't mind. Maybe a summer at Gold Mountain might not be so bad after all.

Dad had chosen our cabin because it was away from the others. He liked privacy when studying or preparing a sermon. Ordinarily Dad is a professor of Old Testament studies. His undergraduate degree was in archaeology. We were in Gold Mountain because Dad was writing a paper and needed quiet; and the church at Gold Mountain was without a pastor, so they had offered him the cabin rent free for the summer. It was an offer he couldn't refuse.

"When I'm finished at the store I'll drop around. And by

8

the way—my name's Joe Greene."

"He's Peter, and I'm Dawn," I said, quickly wiping my hands on my faded jeans and extending a hand.

"Pete Carson," my brother corrected. He didn't like "Peter."

"Maybe I'll bring along my sister, Vicki," Joe called back as he started his motorbike.

"Now why does he have to do that?" Peter was growling as Joe rode away.

"Don't worry," I told him, "Vicki won't come when she hears how rude you are."

"I'm not rude," my brother denied. "I just don't beat around the bush."

"Well, you'd better start beating around the bush and rustle up some kindling to start that old wood stove or there won't be any lunch," Mother told him. She could appear out of nowhere even quicker than Peter. In fact my brother is like my mother in more ways than one. I'm more like my father, not so hasty and impetuous.

"How come I always get the backbreaking little jobs?" Peter demanded. But he went off to search for firewood.

"Do you really think this cabin is haunted?" I asked Dad during lunch.

"What utter nonsense!" Mother exclaimed. "It's the most ridiculous thing I ever heard."

"I'll reserve my opinion until the whole story is in," my father told me. That was his usual position.

Mother said that a person who stood six-feet-four in his bare feet and weighed two hundred and forty, give or take a few pounds, could afford to wait for the full story. People who were only five-feet-two and weighed less than one hundred pounds had better get a quick start or it was apt to be "blotto."

"You can tell Joe to keep his ghosts away from this cabin," Mother told me. She sounded a little grumpy. Maybe that was because she was having so much trouble with the old cabin cookstove. It wouldn't draw properly. She said there were probably bird's nests in the chimney, and she suggested that Father take a look.

Father agreed that it might be a good idea, but said that he wanted to be sure all of the young birds had graduated—learned to fly—before he disturbed any nests in the stone chimney.

9

"I think it's neat," Peter said. His mouth was full, and Mother made him wait till he had finished chewing his hot dog before he went on. "We've only been here a few hours, and already we have a ghost and a lost mine to look for."

"You're forgetting the rock concert that is coming next Saturday." There were posters all around the village announcing the "Mountain Rogues" and the coming rock concert.

Mother rolled her eyes. "And I thought we were coming to the mountains for a little peace and quiet."

"A ghost and a lost mine," Father mused, as if to change the subject. "I wonder how they tie together?"

"I'll let you know as soon as I solve the case," Peter said.

The man at the office where we had picked up our key to the cabin had mentioned the lost mine but not the ghost. He had even offered to sell us a map showing the location of the treasure for a dollar.

Somewhere in the heart of Gold Mountain—the mountain from which the village took its name—there was supposed to be a lost mine. The Indians had known about this mine for a long time, according to the legend. But with the coming of the white man they had filled in the opening—that, or else it had been covered by a rock slide. Anyway it was still lost.

"If anyone knows enough to draw a map, why is the mine still lost?" Mother asked the man with the maps for sale.

The man was evasive and stammered around a bit, but he finally admitted that the map was just one of the area. The red X stamped on the face of Gold Mountain only meant that there was supposed to be a lost mine in the general vicinity.

Mother didn't buy a map.

I asked to be excused because I could see Joe and two girls waiting in the yard. They had just come up. I could see them through the open window, and so could Peter. He made a face and went to the window for a sneak preview.

I told him to come on and went outside.

Joe introduced us all. Joe's sister, Vicki, was the smaller of the two girls. She wore her dark hair short and looked as if she could be a lot of fun. Vicki was also very pretty, with dimples that even my private eye brother would probably appreciate. I thought she was about Peter's age, but it was hard to tell.

The other girl, Gloria Benson, looked older, about my age. Her shoulder-length hair was a reddish brown, like polished mahogany. She wore a flat-topped senorita's hat, tied under her chin. The rest of her costume was Spanish, too, and she wore boots and spurs. She was holding the reins of a beautiful black horse that was pawing at the rocky ground.

I felt suddenly hollow in the pit of my stomach. It was as if my balloon of excitement had been punctured. The new girl was such a picture of smart confidence. Peter would call her "cool."

"Gloria was out riding," Vicki explained, "and she wanted to meet you, so she came along. "She's always on the lookout for horseback-riding companions."

"Do you ride?" Gloria asked. She was giving me a good going over with her blue-green eyes.

"Not really." The queasies were back again. But I managed to sound casual. "I've only been on a horse once in my whole life. I didn't dare tell her how I broke out with the hives afterwards. I was hoping Peter wouldn't remember it and blurt it out in front of everybody.

"What a pity!" Gloria made it sound as if I were some sort of a deprived person. Then she dismissed me with a shrug. "I'd better be rolling," she told Vicki and Joe. "I'm due for a swimming lesson at the hotel pool in an hour." She struck her right boot top with the handle of her riding crop as if the pool date had almost escaped her mind.

"Glad to have met you," I said in an attempt to be polite.

Peter merely grunted. He had scarcely taken his eyes off Vicki.

With an ease that I could not help but envy, Gloria swung to the back of the eager horse. "*Hasta manana!*" she called out. Today she was being completely Spanish.

She started off in a shower of flying gravel and then reined in her horse and rode back. "I almost forgot. I'm in the finals at the hotel swim meet Wednesday—100-meter freestyle and platform diving. If you get a chance, drop around."

Once again she started off, churning up gravel, and this time she kept on going. I hoped that my relief wasn't too noticeable. There was something about Gloria that was over-powering. It was easy to imagine her in a swimming pool, showering the spectators with spray as she led the other swimmers to the finish mark—or doing a perfect swan dive from the high platform. I shut my eyes and trembled at the mere thought of diving off a high board.

Vicki laughed. "Gloria likes to put on a show, but it's always a good one. She'll win the 100-meter freestyle and the diving thing, too. She always does. And someday she'll own just about the whole town of Gold Mountain. She hasn't any brothers or sisters, and her father, Cal Benson, practically owns the air we breath."

"Come along," Joe said. "Let's get started." He seemed anxious to change the subject.

We walked over to the picnic area, where we had a good view of Gold Mountain—the mountain. Having a mountain and a village with the same name was a bit confusing.

"That's the Devil's Brow," Vicki said, pointing to a line of rocks near the very top of the mountain.

"Why the Devil's Brow?" my brother wanted to know.

"Because it looks sort of like a giant brow," Vicki explained. "They say that everytime the devil frowns there is a rock slide. Hope he doesn't frown again soon."

"The devil of the mountain will do more than frown if Cal Benson keeps up his blasting." Joe was frowning, too, but he didn't explain his remark just then.

We moved closer to the mountain along a well-worn trail.

"Look!" Peter gestured. "A copter. Man, would I like to be up there!"

We could hear the steady drum of the helicopter's motor. It seemed headed for the rocky cliffs, but suddenly it made a sweeping turn. It passed directly over our heads and then made another banking turn. This time it came so close that we could see a bearded man at the controls. Beside him was a huge black and tan German shepherd.

"The two beasts!" Vicki exclaimed.

I thought she must be joking until I saw how tightly she had pressed her lips together. Joe looked serious, too.

Peter was the only one who waved at the man and the dog in the helicopter. The pilot jerked his head slightly in response, and the dog bared his teeth.

"Why did they drop so low?" I asked. The helicopter had scuttled away and disappeared.

"Spying," Vicki said grimly. "Hank Woods is as low as they come. And he has trained his dog to be mean and vicious. I saw Nero once with a dead fawn."

"Nero is the dog's name," Joe explained. "I reported the fawn business to a ranger, but Hank claimed the deer was already dead."

"I call Hank 'the spy in the sky,' " Vicki said.

"Why would Hank want to spy on us?" Peter wanted to know.

Before Vicki could explain, Joe changed the subject. "See that streak running up the face of the mountain?"

"Yes." I had noticed the ribbonlike thread. "What is it?"

"That's where Cal Benson's incline railroad will be. Cars pulled by cables will carry folks to his hotel-restaurant on the Brow. His workmen are blasting for the foundation now."

No way would I ride up on that thing, I thought.

I looked but all I could see was a cloud of dust rising from the rocky Brow. It looked like someone was dusting it with a giant powder puff. Afterwards I heard low thunder.

"Blasting," Joe explained. I could tell that he didn't like the idea.

"How come folks let Benson blow up the mountain?" my brother demanded.

"Because he's rich," Vicki said, making a distasteful mouth. "Like I told you, Benson practically owns Gold Mountain village. He owns the big hotel on the road to Marble Mountain. He owns the market where Joe works. He owns the heliport on the Devil's Brow. He owns the helicopter. He owns—"

"He doesn't own the lost gold mine," I reminded her.

"No, my dad would have owned that if he hadn't died of overexertion—a heart attack," Vicki told us soberly.

I guess I showed my surprise. Peter whistled.

"You'd better hear the story from the first," Joe said. So we sat down on some handy boulders.

Chapter Two

"It started with our great-grandfather. When he was a boy, Indians lived freely on the land. They hadn't been put on reservations." Joe paused as if to see if we were still listening.

"Go on—go on," Peter said impatiently. I nudged him to be quiet.

"When my grandfather made a friend of one of the Indians, a very old man, he told him a strange story," Joe continued. "This man was one of three brothers who had been guardians of a great treasure. The cave where the treasure was hidden was on a mountain—'The Mountain of Gold.' "

"They probably stole the treasure from the Spanish or from a California wagon train," my brother blurted out. "That's what they always do in the movies or on TV." He avoided my kick, but Vicki's frown quieted him.

"That's a stereotyped version," Vicki said.

Joe continued. "The old Indian drew an arrow in the dust and told my great-grandfather that it was just such an arrow, cut in a rock, that pointed to the cave's entrance, where the treasure was hidden. And that—"

"You're leaving out the part about one of the brothers falling from a ledge," Vicki interrupted.

"OK. Once while visiting the treasure cave, the oldest brother fell from a rock ledge and was killed. According to tribal tradition, the other brothers couldn't or wouldn't return to the place of his death."

"Why?" Peter wanted to know. I knew why. I didn't blame the brothers. I wouldn't want to go back either. They were probably scared, just like me.

"That's just the way it was. I don't know why," Joe said. "Anyway, the tribe was put on a reservation shortly after that, and the cave and its treasure was forgotten, except by the last living brother, who had been one of the guardians. He told my great-grandfather, and when he grew up he told my grandfather the story."

"Why didn't he ever look for the cave?" Peter never ran out of questions. I'll confess that sometimes I was glad for his questions—questions that I was too afraid to ask.

"They always thought of it as just a story, with little or no truth to it—that is, until Dad," Vicki said.

Joe picked up from there. "Our father was an archaeologist who specialized in American Indian cultures—especially the Rocky Mountain tribes."

"Wow, that's a coincidence," I almost shouted. "Our father majored in archaeology too, before he went to the seminary. He was mostly interested in Middle Eastern work."

Vicki smiled. "We do have a lot in common. I knew we were a lot alike in a lot of ways."

"Can we get on with the story?" Peter sighed. "The suspense is killing me."

"Dad taught at Western University until his health broke down," Joe said. "That's partly the reason we came to Gold Mountain two years ago to live.

"Well—Dad had a little artifact, a figure of a cleverly shaped panther made out of pure gold. He had found it years before while digging around an ancient Indian burial mound. Dad thought it might prove that the forefathers of many Rocky Mountain Indian tribes were advanced far beyond the common belief. He wrote a paper for an archaeological journal stating his theory." Joe added: "A panther is the same as a mountain lion or cougar."

"But other archaeologists laughed at him. They said that the golden panther was probably brought up from Mexico or Central America by Spanish explorers—or some such thing." Vicki had taken over again. "Some day Dad will be proven right."

"Maybe," Joe said. "But to get back to the lost mine—Dad had heard about the local mine legend, of course. And as long as he was spending the summer at Gold Mountain, he thought he might as well scout around a bit. He remembered the story

15

told to his great-grandfather and it seemed possible the two legends had the same origin. If there actually was a mine or treasure cave it might prove to be the source of the gold used in the golden panther."

"Dad wasn't supposed to do anything very strenuous," Vicki put in, "because of his weakened heart. That's why he hired Zeke Woods to drive him around in his jeep." She paused and looked at Joe.

"Why don't you take over," Joe told her. "I'm out of air pressure."

You could tell that Joe didn't like long-winded speeches.

"We don't really know what happened that last day," Vicki said. "Dad left early in the morning with Zeke Woods in the jeep. He came home late, and Joe and I were already asleep. In the morning mother told us that Dad's heart had stopped beating sometime during the night."

"But he had made some sort of a discovery." Joe had taken over again. "During the night he must have got out of bed and sat at the kitchen table. There were ink stains on the table, and a crude sketch on a scrap torn from a brown grocery sack. There was an arrow with a broken shaft. It was set in the top of a rock and pointed to an opening in some other rocks. These rocks were marked 'Door to Treasure Cave.' That was all."

"How much Zeke Woods knew about Dad's discovery we don't know," Vicki put in. "Zeke was killed a month later in a traffic accident. But his son Hank is very much alive." She made a face. "Before he died Zeke must have told Hank about driving Dad around. And about the golden panther." About 6 months after Dad's death Hank came here to work for Mr. Benson.

"That was a mistake Dad made," Joe said. "He was proud of the little artifact and showed it to people. I guess he thought someone might give him a tip that would help him find other artifacts to help him prove his theory about the advanced Indian culture."

"I'd like to see the golden panther," Peter said.

"Then you'll have to ask Hank," Vicki told my brother grimly. "One day when no one was home, our house was ransacked. Nothing was taken except Dad's golden panther."

"Of course we don't really know it was Hank," Joe said.

Vicki scoffed. "Who else? Hank's father probably told

Hank about the panther, and he thinks it came from the lost mine. Ever since then he has been spying on us. Thinks we'll lead him to the treasure cave."

"But how big is the panther?" Peter wanted to know.

"Only about two and a half inches long and an inch high," Joe said. "That's a lot of gold but the main value is as an artifact. Dad was sure there must be others and that they were used as burial pieces. They were probably kept in a cave storehouse."

Peter got up and turned a flip. "Why don't we just ransack Hank's place and get the panther back?"

"You don't just break into someone's home—unless you're somebody like Hank," Vicki said. "Besides, you saw Hank's dog. Nero would tear an intruder to pieces. Anyway, Hank has the panther well hidden; you can be sure of that."

"Hank was a pilot in the marine corps, and since his discharge he has been working for Benson, flying his copter," Joe said.

"It gives him a good chance to spy on us," Vicki put in.

Joe rose and stretched. "We'd better be heading back, or your folks will start worrying."

"Just one cotton pickin' minute!" my brother exclaimed. What about that ghost story? How come our cabin is haunted?"

"I'll give you the gruesome details on the way back," Joe replied with his broad grin.

"I told you it was just a campfire story, and it really is," Joe told us, as we started back. "According to the local legend, the only white man who was supposed to have seen the inside of the treasure cave, or lost mine, until our dad came into the picture was supposed to have a cabin where yours now stands. The story is that the Indians did away with him and burned his cabin. Those Indians are dead and gone, but their ghosts still haunt the place to make sure none of the present-day explorers bother their treasure.

"Any way you look at it, the ghost business is silly," Peter said. He seemed anxious that I didn't take the story too seriously. Goose bumps were rising on the back of my arm. Everything I'd heard just made those old queasies churn more and more in my stomach. Cave—Indians—ghosts—dogs and men in helicopters—it was just too much for an Olympic coward like me.

My new friends had a wild story alright. And somehow I didn't like being in the middle. But I liked them. They were fun to be around.

O God, why am I such a fraidycat? I thought to myself.

Suddenly Vicki remembered something. "Hey, there's going to be an Indian dance tonight. Do you think you can come?"

Joe added: "There will be Indian dancers at the Gathering Place."

"Chief Manitaw brings a group of dancers here every summer," Vicki said.

"I'll bet they're looking for the lost treasure." Peter sounded excited. "I mean—I'll bet they're guarding it."

"Joe has tried talking to Chief Manitaw about the lost Indian mine, or cave," Vicki told us.

"Manitaw says he never heard of a lost Indian mine or treasure cave in these parts," Joe said.

I was listening but not saying much. That was usual when I was trying to handle my fear. Peter is the private investigator in our family.

On the way home we went by Joe and Vicki's house. Their mother was at work, but we met Black Bart, a pet raccoon. They had found him in some brush at the base of Gold Mountain when he was very young.

Black Bart looked like a little masked bandit with his eye patches. And he acted the part. He kept trailing me around and tried to sneak his slender little fingers into the pockets of my jacket. Joe finally had to collar Bart, but he seemed glad that their pet liked me.

When we parted it was with the promise to meet again that evening. Vicki was allowed to attend the dances if Joe was along. I was almost certain that Mother would have no objections to me and Peter joining them.

"Just don't get scalped," Dad teased. "I wouldn't want you to lose that beautiful head of hair."

My hair isn't really beautiful. It is sort of the color of taffy candy before it has been pulled too much. Just the same, I gave him an extra hug for making me feel more glamorous. My father has a way of doing that for me.

Chapter Three

I had never seen an Indian dance except in the movies or on TV. It was exciting but—as usual—scary. The Indians all looked so grim. From what I had read in my history books I guessed they had good reasons to look that way.

Peter and Vicki were enjoying themselves, but Joe looked sleepy.

When the dancers stopped for a break, Joe suggested that he and Peter get us some pop. We took up a collection.

Just then a sleek red sports car with its top down came swishing up to the gathering place. The man at the wheel had a thick black beard. The girl beside him was Gloria Benson. Even before I saw Nero erect on the back seat, tongue hanging out, big white teeth gleaming, I knew that the bearded man was Hank Woods.

"Cal Benson won't let Gloria go anywhere after dark unless Hank and Nero are along," Vicki confided, "and she doesn't like him any more than we do."

"I'd feel safer at home," I said. I felt a twinge of sympathy for Gloria. How could she stand being around that dog?

"She doesn't like the dog either, but Nero is safe as long as Hank is around.—Shhh! She's coming over."

Gloria's thick reddish-brown hair was tied back with a blue ribbon. She had been playing tennis and still had on her tennis costume. It showed off her long, smoothly tanned legs to advantage. I'll bet she's proud of them, I thought. And then I was ashamed of my thought.

She gave me a brief nod of recognition and turned to Vicki. "Sorry, I'll have to break our riding date tomorrow. Something came up." She made a gesture with her hand. "That's the curse of belonging to a hotel. Your time is never your own."

"It's OK," Vicki said. "I'm still sore from the last ride."

Joe and my brother returned with the pop, and Joe offered to go for another bottle. One for Gloria.

"Thanks no, darling. I'm in training for the swim meet—remember. But I'll take a rain check." She patted Joe's arm, and he looked embarrassed.

For no good reason that I could think of I wanted to shake Gloria. It wasn't like me. I was usually too chicken.

"There's your father and mother!" Vicki cried suddenly.

I was glad for the interruption.

Chief Manitaw came over and invited my father to join them in the next dance. And sure enough, when the next dance started, my father was in the lineup.

The dance wasn't nearly so scary with my own father in the circle. But I was a bit embarrassed. Father was at least a head taller than the tallest Indian.

Gloria turned to me, and I read amusement in her green eyes. "No wonder your dad's a minister. He can reach right up to heaven and get instructions from God personally."

If anyone else had said it I would have thought it was funny.

"Your dad is a good sport," Joe told me. I was glad that he wasn't grinning.

Gloria and her escorts finally left, and the air seemed to be fresher.

For a finale, Chief Manitaw produced a bow and a dozen arrows. The tips of the arrows had been dipped in pitch. After they were lighted he shot them one by one into the night. They made fiery arcs like tiny rockets. Of course the arrows were directed so as to fall on bare ground in an open area. The ones that did not burn out in flight were soon put out by willing helpers.

Tomorrow was Saturday, and Joe would be tied down at the village market all day. But Sunday after church services we could take a real hike—if our parents were willing.

"We'll make a picnic of it and go to Indian Springs," Vicki said. "Then, if we're spotted by the 'spy in the sky,' he won't be suspicious. Actually we'll be looking for the arrow on the rock."

"Sure," Peter agreed. "We'll take along a shovel and a pick

and start a mine shaft. Then, while Hank is watching that hole, some of us will sneak away and find the real mine. That's the way the ground squirrels trick the bluejays."

Vicki dimpled. "Peter—what an idea! Hank Woods is a lot smarter than a jay. He knows the mine we are looking for is back in the rocks somewhere. Sort of a cave. Everyone in Gold Mountain knows that."

"That's not a bad idea, Peter," Joe told my brother. "We'll keep it in mind."

That was one of the nice things about Joe, I was beginning to discover. He never put people down, even if their suggestions were far out, like my brother's were apt to be.

That night I lay awake for a long time, thinking. I thought about Joe and Vicki's father. What a tragedy his death had been to the family.

Vicki had told me that her mother had decided to stay on in Gold Mountain because they all loved the wildlife and the beauty of the valley. But it was Vicki's secret belief that her mother hoped that one day they might make a discovery that would prove their father's theory about the origin of the golden panther. They might even find the same cave he had found on that tragic last day.

Joe had secured a job as a delivery boy at the local market. He worked after school and Saturdays till summer vacation, and then full time. Vicki kept house while their mother worked in the Gold Mountain bakery. They both seemed so responsible, so sure of themselves. I liked them both, and I liked them more and more as we became friends. How lucky I was, I thought. I'd dreaded coming to Gold Mountain, but everyday I liked it more and more. I was even getting used to seeing wild animals cross my path. No longer did I shriek or run helter-skelter away from them.

Finally I fell asleep.

I woke trembling with dread. A hand was clutching my foot. Probably in the other hand was a scalping knife. My scream sent the ghostly something springing through the open window. It seemed to me that it wore a feathered headdress. Dad reached me first.

The sight of his familiar bulk was reassuring.

"Was it a ghost?" Dad asked. He seemed to understand, because he was smiling.

I could only nod silently. Although I had not been thinking about the legend of the Indian ghosts consciously, they must have been lurking in some corner of my brain, waiting to jump at me as soon as I let my defenses down.

Dad walked slowly over to the open window. He squeezed his shoulders into the opening and peered into the night. Then he pried himself loose and left the room.

When he returned he was leading Black Bart, Joe's pet raccoon. "He seems to be house trained, and more of a pet than a wild animal."

"It belongs to my new friends, Joe and Vicki. I guess he came to visit me," I said wiping my eyes.

Dad hugged me. "He won't hurt you," he said.

"I know—I know." My hands were still shaking. "O Dad, why am I so afraid all the time?"

Dad took a seat on the side of the bed. "Dawn, being afraid is not altogether a bad thing. Some things should be feared. There are two kinds of fear: rational and irrational. Fear of things that happen suddenly, fear of going to an unfamiliar place—that is normal, and most people have this kind of fear. Total lack of fear is as bad as being frightened of everything. Now, fear can be overcome, but it takes faith. I am often afraid. I've been in difficult situations, but I know I'm never alone. I always have God with me, and Jesus is a constant companion. Knowing that I'm not alone, and knowing that I'm not in the situation all alone, makes me able to face the problem and overcome the fear. Remember that.

"Instead of asking God why you are afraid, ask Him to help you handle your fear and to overcome it with His help."

I felt somewhat relieved. Black Bart insisted on staying with me. Suddenly he didn't look like a wild animal, but a regular house pet, not much different from a cat. He crawled to the foot of my bed and went to sleep.

Slowly I relaxed, but I kept my light on just a little longer. "Dear God," I prayed quietly, "help me not to be so afraid."

Chapter Four

Sunday came. Dad held a service in the little church surrounded by tall pine. Four tiny birds sat on the window sill and observed us with black eyes. Once during the service Black Bart wandered to the side door and stood on his hind legs, begging for Dad to give him a sugar lump. That's how Dad had gotten him to come in the night before. Dad sure had an unusual congregation for his first sermon at Gold Mountain.

During service I watched Mom. She was sitting up very straight and paying attention—just as if Dad were not related and she were hearing him for the first time. I know she felt proud of Dad—we all were—but when the button popped off her jacket, I couldn't help but giggle. Mom was literally bursting with pride.

The button fell to the floor, and I picked it up. Mother didn't have any pockets in her jacket, so she motioned for me to keep it for her. I was wearing my lime-colored suede jacket, my current favorite. So I slipped it into one of my pockets.

We sang "Take Time to Be Holy," and then the church service was over.

Joe and Vicki were waiting for us in the rear of the seating section. It was the first opportunity we had to introduce our new friends to our parents. Dad was still busy shaking hands.

Vicki noticed the unusual brass buttons on my mother's jacket and asked her about them.

"They're from Dawn's grandfather's naval uniform. There are supposed to be six of them on my jacket but one popped off during church. Dawn is keeping it for me," Mother said.

We said good-bye to Mother and hit the trail. Joe was carrying a backpack that held about everything. He told me that he even had some antisnakebite serum, so not to worry about snakes. I hadn't till then. My first impulse was to fake a headache and not go. But I talked myself out of it. Snakes! We all carried sack lunches. Vicki and Joe had walkie-talkies.

"They don't have much range, but we can keep in touch," Vicki told us.

I felt like a tenderfoot, because I was the only one who was not wearing jeans. My green slacks and low-heeled heavy-soled shoes didn't seem as appropriate as they had when I left the cabin for church. That was the main reason I wasn't wearing jeans—Mother didn't like me to wear them to church, even on vacation. Peter was wearing his Little League baseball cap and even his freckles looked excited.

I could hear Vicki and Peter laughing up ahead, but still Vicki called her brother on the walkie-talkie.

"Chipmunk calling Tall Bear—Chipmunk calling—"

"This is Tall Bear," Joe responded. "Come in, Chipmunk."

"No spy in the sky," she said.

"Do you think Hank really spies on you?" I asked Joe.

"Yes and no. Hank works for Cal Benson. He flies Benson to and from the Devil's Brow and anywhere else he wants to go. Being in the air so much does give Hank a good chance to keep tab on things. He'd probably know if anyone was headed for Rocky Meadows."

"What's special about Rocky Meadows?" I asked.

"It may be the place Hank's father drove my dad that last day. There are lots or rocks and rock caves there. Zeke Woods could have driven his jeep to Stony Point, and Dad could have hiked to the Meadows from there. Hank would probably know if his father did drive Dad there."

"Will we go there today—to the Meadows?" I asked.

Joe shook his head. "Too far. We need to get an early start to get to the Meadows and back in one day, and still have time to look around. Indian Springs is a nice easy hike. You need to get acclimated."

"That sounds like a fifty-dollar word."

Joe laughed. "It means to get used to the altitude."

"That's what I thought it meant. But I'm already used to the altitude, and I like it," I told him.

"We'll see. We're pretty high here." Joe pointed. "See the snow on those high peaks?"

I nodded and was about to speak when I heard a crunching of gravel on the trail we had just covered. It was as if someone was trying to overtake us. Then I heard a big dog panting.

My heart was pounding as I spun about. Joe had turned too, and now he stepped in front of me. Hank Woods and his dog, Nero, came around a bend of the trail and were only a few feet away. Hank was wearing jeans and a blue sports shirt.

It was the first time I had seen Hank Woods and his dog at such close range. My backbone felt as if it had just gone into deep freeze.

Hank had an ugly scar on his right cheek that his beard didn't hide, and his eyes were red-rimmed pools of ice water. Nero frightened me even more—he was drooling and showing his ugly teeth. I thought of the dead fawn.

Despite the menacing Hank and the snarling Nero, Joe held his ground. He carried a pronged stick that he said was for emergency use. Joe held the stick slightly in front of him as he awaited Hank's move.

Hank said something to Nero and the dog sat down on his haunches, but he was still slobbering and whining.

"Where are you kids headed?" Hank sounded as if he was questioning some prisoner. I thought my heart was going to pound right out of my chest. Please don't faint, I said to myself.

Joe hesitated a moment and then he said calmly, "If it's any of your business we're headed for Indian Springs for a picnic."

"Picnic!" Hank sounded as if he didn't believe it. He moved a step closer, and Nero got up from his haunches with a snarl. "I think you kids are looking for that lost Indian mine. If you find it, just remember that it already belongs to me. I've got proof of that. Your dad was trying to cheat my old man, but he failed. I was in the marine corps but—"

"That's a lie—about Dad trying to cheat your father!" Vicki had come running back along the trail with Peter at her heels. Now she ranged herself alongside of her brother. I couldn't detect one ounce of fear.

"The only thing you've got is the golden panther you stole when you ransacked our house." Vicki's cheeks were flaming. "And we want it back!"

26

"Better not make any accusations you can't prove," Hank said. His voice had a menacing softness.

"Someday we will prove it!" Vicki's cheeks had lost their color. She looked as pale as the snow on the distant peaks, but she held her ground.

Hank sneered. "Don't get any ideas of prowling around my place. "Nero is trained to kill."

Joe said evenly: "We know—deer."

"My dog doesn't kill deer, I proved that to the satisfaction of the park ranger, but he might kill a prowler. Nero's a guard dog. And there's no law against that."

"Unless he's guarding stolen property," Vicki said hotly. Some of her red color had returned. "We know you—"

Joe motioned for her to stop talking.

Hank gave a nasty laugh. "This is just a warning. I'm going to get that gold. Don't you kids forget that!" Then he spoke to Nero, and man and dog started back down the trail. Soon they were hidden from view.

Joe was the first to speak. "We aren't going to let Hank spoil our picnic, are we?"

"What makes me mad," Vicki said, "is that I've always liked dogs. I've never been afraid of one before. But Hank has trained Nero to be mean. It's not the dog's fault."

"Come along!" Joe said. "Let's get started."

I managed to get one foot in front of the other. I guess I was doing a good job of covering up my feelings again, because Vicki said, "Dawn, I'm so glad you and Peter were with us. I'm so glad to have a friend like you."

Wow! Her glad to have me as a friend! I was just thinking how brave she had been. "Weren't you scared?" I asked.

"You'd better believe it. Hank and that beast scare me to death."

"You didn't act afraid."

"I put on a good act."

"I know what you mean," I said. She had no idea how much I did know what she meant.

The trail went so close to the river that we had to yell to make ourselves heard. They called Gold River a river, but that was bragging. It was more like a noisy, rushing creek.

We turned away from Gold River, and the trail became much steeper. Vicki and Peter bounded ahead.

They were waiting for us where the trail divided.

"That water's so noisy I was afraid you couldn't understand me over the walkie-talkie," Vicki told Joe. "Are we headed for Indian Springs?"

"Yes, we can eat lunch there. While we eat I'll show Dawn and Peter the sketch Dad left of the arrow on the rock."

"Great!" said Peter as he and Vicki started up the trail again. "We'll meet you there."

"Watch out for snakes!" Joe called after them.

I laughed nervously. Snakes! The queasies started again. I fought back this time. It was a lovely day that even my fears couldn't spoil. The smell of pines and firs made you think you could never get enough fresh air into your lungs. Joe used his forked stick to point out certain flowers and trees. He knew the names of a lot of them and sometimes interesting facts.

"That's a lodgepole pine," he told me, pointing to one of the pines that stood along the trail like soldiers on parade. "They call them that because the tree furnished Indians with tepee poles."

"You sure know a lot about wild things," I said with admiration.

"Not as much as I'd like to know," Joe replied. "This valley holds a hundred and forty kinds of wild grass and more than three hundred plants. Wish I could identify all of them."

I finally saw a flower that I knew and pointed to it. "That's a columbine—Colorado's state flower."

Joe got it for me. "I don't think one flower will be missed," he said, handing it to me.

It was a lovely icy-blue color and looked like a small buttercup. I wrapped it in a fold of tissue to keep for my memory book.

The strange antics of a small chipmunk caught my attention. I noticed that I didn't start when I saw a spider or a strange bug.

"Black Bart has been sleeping at the foot of my bed for the past few nights. I hope you don't mind," I said.

"So that's where that little rascal has been. No, I don't mind at all. He's always been free to come and go. I'm glad he likes you. He has good taste."

I guess I blushed. My face felt red, if it wasn't.

Suddenly I saw a hawk against a rock cliff, and it

reminded me of Hank and his helicopter—the spy in the sky.

"Since Hank wasn't up in his copter today, how did he know we were on the trail?" I asked Joe.

"He was out with Nero and just happened to spot us. When he isn't up in the chopper he's usually out with his dog."

"Did Hank ever actually follow you when he spotted you from the air?" I asked Joe.

"Twice. Both times I had borrowed the motorbike from the market. The first time I took off for Stony Point on a weekday—my day off. I parked the bike at Stony Point and started along the trail to Rocky Meadows. Right off the bat Hank was over me in his copter. It was uncanny."

"Maybe he knew that you had borrowed the bike. Maybe someone at the market told him. Vicki said that the market belongs to Cal Benson."

Joe shook his head. "Nobody at the market likes Hank."

"Can we go to Rocky Meadows on our next hike?" Excitement overtook my senses. What had I just said? Surely this wasn't the Dawn I knew. Maybe that was it—I wasn't the same old afraid-of-everything Dawn.

"Are you sure you want to help us look for the lost Indian cave—now that you've met Hank and Nero?" Joe was looking at me closely.

No, no, the old Dawn screamed out inside of me. I said, "I'm sure." Then I added to myself, *"God, please help me not to be afraid.*

"OK, if you're sure. We can—" Joe broke off.

Once again Vicki was calling Joe on her walkie-talkie. Only this time her voice sounded urgent. "Joe! 10-33—10-33! Quick!"

"Vicki needs help!" Joe started running along the trail, and I followed as quickly as I could.

When we caught up with Vicki and Peter I froze in my tracks. Peter was perched on a rock shelf about 15 feet above us. In front of him was a rattler, coiled and ready to strike. Vicki watched pale-faced and helpless, but somehow I went into action. I mounted the same rock shelf, but on the opposite side of the rattler.

"Don't move," Joe cautioned Peter. He was circling to the left.

I felt like I was outside myself—watching somebody else in

my body. From somewhere I was getting the strength to do what I had to do. My brother was in danger. If I didn't act, he could get hurt. That one thought kept me going.

Joe was sliding his feet carefully forward. In his right hand he held his pronged stick. I was right behind Peter now, softly reminding him to stay still.

When Joe was close enough to attract the snake's attention, he teased it with his stick. When the snake angrily struck at the wood, Joe used the prongs to pin the rattler to the ledge. At the same time I pulled Peter backward and away from the snake. In case Joe missed, Peter would at least be out of striking distance.

Weak with relief, I helped Peter down from the rock shelf. He squirmed away from me and jumped.

"I could have handled it," he said, red with embarrassment. I didn't need to be rescued."

"Enough!" I said to my brother. I rarely pulled rank or age on my brother, but this was one time I wasn't going to put up with his smart-mouthing. "You did a foolish thing by leaving the path. Joe and Vicki are used to this area. You aren't. There are dangers out here, and you need to be more cautious from now on."

"Lighten up on him," Joe said. "He'll be more careful next time, I'm sure." He turned to Peter. "Remember to stay on the beaten path from now on, OK?"

Peter nodded his head.

Chapter Five

By the time we reached Indian Springs I was completely out of breath. Joe glanced back at me and grinned. "I thought you were used to the altitude."

"It isn't the altitude that bothers me—it's the thin air," I told him.

We all laughed. It really is harder to climb when you can't get enough oxygen.

A number of hikers ahead of us were already eating their lunches. There was one empty table away from the others, and we took it.

"That rotten egg smell comes from the sulphur in the springs," Joe explained for my benefit.

Vicki and Peter were holding their noses, but when we started to eat our sandwiches and potato chips they forgot about the sulphur smell.

"Why is it called Indian Springs?" I asked. "Did the Indians discover it?"

Joe nodded. "Probably—a long time ago. For longer than anyone can remember they came here and drank the water. They thought it was good medicine."

After we had finished eating our lunches and fed the scraps to the chipmunks and ground squirrels and the jays, Joe got out a ragged slip of brown paper from his pack. It was the sketch his father had left of the arrow on the rock, the marker to the Lost Indian Mine.

There was not a great deal to see. An arrow drawn on a flat rock. Or rather the arrow was set into the rock. It had a break in its shaft. A dotted line had been drawn from the arrow marker to three standing rocks. Between two of the large boulders there was an opening. The opening was marked "Door to Treasure Cave." On one side of the doorway was a dwarfed pine tree.

"That cave entrance might be anywhere on Gold Mountain where there are large standing rocks," Joe said ruefully. "But the rocks in Dad's sketch seem to look more like the ones you find at Rocky Meadows."

"Then why haven't you looked there?" Peter asked.

"A good question," Joe approved in his usual unruffled tone.

Before her brother could offer to explain, Vicki took over. "For one thing, Joe's been tied down at the market. And for another thing, we're just getting old enough so Mom will let us hike without a whole bunch going along. And for still another thing—you tell him, Joe."

Joe laughed. "We have been to Rocky Meadows a few times but never alone. And never when we had much chance to look around. The Meadows covers a lot of ground, and by the time you hike up the trail your time is about gone."

"There are a zillion caves and crevices." Vicki took over. "By the time you examined all of them you'd have been dead for a hundred years."

"If you didn't fall off a ledge, like the Indian in your great-grandfather's story," I reminded with a shiver.

"The arrow on the rock may not point to a cave at all," Joe said. "In my great-grandfather's story it was called a 'treasure cave.' Dad marked the opening in the rocks 'Door to Treasure Cave.' But folks around here talk about the 'Lost Indian Mine.' They may be one and the same thing and they may not be. Indians didn't often work mines. But if the golden panther was really the work of ancient Indians who lived in the Rocky Mountains, it proves that they did work mines. They also refined or smelted gold."

"Dad was hoping to find a treasure cave or Indian storehouse, and not a gold mine," Vicki said. "He wasn't interested in the formations. He was trying to find another artifact made of gold or any other metal that would prove his archaeological theory."

"What difference does it make?" Peter wanted to know. "Why do you care if it's a mine with a vein of ore or a cave?"

"If the gold is in artifacts, then it's treasure trove," Joe said. "I want to find the cave to preserve a culture or help prove that my father's work wasn't in vain. Hank wants it strictly for the money, and he'd just as soon melt down centuries-old artifacts and destroy historical evidence as to breathe."

"In the olden days treasure trove belonged to the king unless the original owner was found." I was proud to be able to add something to the conversation.

"Right," Joe said. "But in the United Sates the right of the state or federal government is seldom claimed. Treasure trove belongs to the finder if the original owner isn't known. Archaelogical finds are usually claimed by a school, a museum, or whoever funds the archaeologist's digs. There are very few individuals who can afford to spend the time and money looking for treasure."

"What I really hope is that the treasure cave proves to be both—a mine and a storehouse," Vicki said. "Then maybe we can prove Dad's theory and have a gold mine, too."

"To get back to Dad's sketch." Joe tapped the ragged piece of brown paper sack with his forefinger. "It doesn't tell us much, but at least we know what sort of an arrow to look for. Nobody else even knows about the arrow."

"How about Hank?" It was one question that I was glad to have Peter ask.

"I don't believe Hank Woods knows about the arrow," Joe said. "I was carrying Dad's sketch in my billfold when our house was ransacked. I'd been studying it to see if we had overlooked any clues."

"Hank doesn't know about the arrow on the rock, but I'll bet he thinks we have some sort of a map," Vicki said. "That's why he spies on us. He thinks we'll lead him to the mine. But he can't watch us all the time."

Joe tucked away his father's sketch, and we hiked a little farther along the trail towards Rocky Meadows. We came to a lookout point where we had a good view of the valley.

"I could throw a rock and hit our cabin," Peter bragged.

"It isn't as close as it looks," Vicki told him. "The clear air just makes it look that way."

"Even when you get to Rocky Meadows it really isn't too far from the valley floor," Joe said. "If you're a crow or up in a helicopter. Rocky Meadows is just about a thousand feet above the river. But the trail winds around so much that it takes about three hours steady climbing to get there."

"Unless you're coming from Stony Point. Then it only takes about half an hour. But it's really a rough trail," Vicki told us. "That's the way Dad must've hiked to the Meadows that last day, if he really went there. And that's why it was such a strain on his weak heart."

We were all silent for a moment as we thought about Mr. Greene.

The silence was broken by Vicki, who pointed her finger at a big bird that was no longer a bird. We could hear the drum of the helicopter's motor, although it was soon hidden from our sight by towering pillars of rock.

"The spy in the sky wants to make sure we aren't on the trail to Rocky Meadows. I wish we were!" Vicki exclaimed with her dark eyes flashing.

"We'll get an early start when we tackle it," I was surprised to hear myself say. I was even more surprised by how excited I felt at the prospect. The fear of Hank Woods and his dog had been momentarily shoved into the background.

"Tuesday is my regular day off," Joe said. "If we start early enough we should be able to get to the Meadows before lunch. That will give us a couple of hours to really look around—if it's OK with your folks."

Joe was looking at me as he spoke, but it was my brother who answered him. "It will be," Peter assured him.

Because it had been our first real hike, Peter and I were both tired and went to bed soon after dinner.

I awoke from a dream in which I was being chased by Indians. And while I ran I was trying to scoop up gold nuggets from the floor of a cave. The nuggets were too heavy for me to lift, and at last one of the Indians had me by the shoulder.

The Indian turned out to be Peter shaking me. "Wake up, Dawn! It's the Indians this time sure. The ghosts, I mean. One of them is trying to open my window." My brother was making wavering circles on the floor with his flashlight.

My first thought was of Black Bart. That gave me the courage to throw on my robe and go to investigate. It turned out to be a pine tree branch scraping against the window pane each time it was blown by a gust of wind.

"I knew it all the time," Peter told me. His courage had

returned with a rush. "Think I don't know a rubbing branch when I hear it? I just wanted to see if you knew. Give you some practice in being alert. It'll come in handy when the ghosts really do come."

"Well, thanks a million!" I gave him a push towards his bed.

I was thinking just before I feel asleep that maybe I wasn't such a chicken after all. Sure I was scared when Hank and Nero stopped us on the path, but, like Dad had told me, that was rational fear. There was real danger; it was OK to be afraid. The snake was frightening, and it was rational to be afraid. But I had overcome my fear and done something that two weeks ago I thought I'd never be able to do. Snakes in a book used to make me break out in a cold sweat. I realize now that that was irrational fear. There was no reason for me to be afraid of a picture; it could do me no harm. The live snake in the woods was real and dangerous. I should have been afraid. My brother needed to learn that lesson, too.

Dawn, I said to myself, you're gonna be alright. Just don't get too overconfident, the old Dawn said. "Thanks, God, for helping me with my fear—the irrational fear." Then I fell asleep.

Chapter Six

"No hike tomorrow," Peter told me. "Joe can't get away. He has to fill in for a guy who's sick."

It meant that we would be unable to plan another hike before the following Sunday at the earliest. And it was hard to get an early start on a Sunday, because we were expected to attend church service.

Suddenly I made up my mind that I was going to hike to Rocky Meadows the next day, just as we had planned. It wouldn't be exactly as we had planned either. Joe and Vicki and my brother wouldn't be with me. My father would have to serve as their substitute. Peter had already informed me that he was playing tennis with Vicki in the morning. She was trying to teach him that a tennis racket was not supposed to be swung like a baseball bat.

Dad was willing to hike with me. In fact, he seemed pleased to be asked. "Everyone should have a mountaintop experience at least once in his or her life," he said.

"I'm close enough to the mountaintop experience right here in this cabin," Mother told him, "if you mean an experience in primitive living. I didn't know that anyone cooked on wood stoves anymore."

"Joe said we ought to have a map of the trail," I said. "I can pick one up in the morning when I go for the mail. We can start our hike as soon as I get back."

Early the next morning I walked into the village, which was about a mile from our cabin. I stopped at the post office and the telegraph office. Center City was looking for a new minister to fill their pulpit, and my father had been interviewed. No decision had been made, and father was still hopeful. There weren't any letters or messages, so I went on to the general store.

Mrs. Breedlove, the manager, was behind the counter. Vicki had told me that she was the biggest gossip in Gold Mountain, so I was cautious.

"I want a map that shows the hiking trails," I told her. "Especially the one to Rocky Meadows."

Mrs. Breedlove was sitting on a stool, and she motioned for me to get a map out of the holder on the counter top.

"That one shows most of the valley hiking trails," she told me. She gave me a sharp look. "What are you going to Rocky Meadows for? Figure on finding the Lost Indian Mine?"

She took me by surprise, and I couldn't help giving a start. But when I answered her I tried to sound completely disinterested. "Is that where the lost mine is supposed to be?"

Mrs. Breedlove moved her thick shoulders. "Who knows? I thought maybe you had a special tip from Joe Greene since you've been running around with him and his sister. Some say his dad and Zeke Woods actually found the mine. Both of them dead now. Still one of them must've left some clues."

"Just hiking with my father," I told her airily.

I fancied that Mrs. Breedlove eyed me rather suspiciously as I paid her fifty cents for the map and left the store. Just as I was taking the trail to our cabin I happened to look over my shoulder. It looked as if a red sports car had just driven into the parking space by the general store, but it was too far away for me to tell who was driving. It might have been Hank or it might have been Cal Benson. It didn't seem too important at the time.

Finally we were on our way. I didn't tell Dad that I was planning for us to hike all the way to Rocky Meadows. But I knew he wouldn't mind. My father loved to hike. Mother had fixed our lunch while I was in the village getting the mail.

Dad carried our lunch in an old-fashioned khaki-colored knapsack. The knapsack also held his notebooks and pencils. He never went anywhere without his writing tools.

Crested bluejays gave us a noisy escort as we left Gold River and headed for Indian Springs. Before the pines and aspens closed in I surveyed the sky. I had thought that I heard a faint drumming sound.

A few minutes later Hank Woods came spinning across the trail in his helicopter. He passed almost directly overhead and then scuttled off towards the Devil's Brow. He was following his usual course to the heliport beyond the Brow. Hank was probably on business for his boss. It seemed unlikely that he would be suspicious of two lone hikers, a minister and his daughter. But my father presented a target that would be hard to miss if Hank was on a spying mission. Then I forgot about the copter because Dad had spotted a deer.

The doe was only in sight for a few seconds and then crashed away. But I was excited because it was my first.

"I wish I had brought my camera," I said.

Dad laughed. "You would have had to be fast on the trigger to get that one." You could tell that Dad was enjoying himself. When he filled his lungs with the fresh pure air you could almost hear the rush of the wind as it moved in to close the vacuum he created. Dad had to keep slowing down because his stride was almost double mine. And I am supposed to be a tall girl.

We passed through Indian Springs and I pointed out the picnic table where we had eaten our lunches two days before. At the rate we were traveling we would reach Rocky Meadows well before noon.

The pace began to tell on me. My new boots felt stiff and uncomfortable. They were wearing blisters on my heels. I began to complain. "My feet hurt!"

Dad made me sit down on a handy boulder. Then he opened his knapsack and took out a pair of my heavy-soled but thoroughly broken-in shoes. "Try these on for size," he said with a grin.

"Dad, you're something else! How did you know?"

"I've been hiking with you before," he told me dryly.

After Dad had helped me switch boots for shoes we continued our hike. Our speed had been slowed, because the higher we climbed the more difficult it became to breathe. I had found that out on our Sunday hike with Joe and Vicki. The map called it five miles to Rocky Meadows from Indian Springs but it seemed twice as far. I was hot and I took off my lime-colored jacket. Dad offered to carry it but I told him it wasn't that heavy.

There were larger rocks along the trail now. Some of them

upended, just like the rocks had been in the sketch left by Joe and Vicki's father.

We came to a weathered sign tacked to a pine. In barely distinguishable lettering it said that we had reached ROCKY MEADOWS. It wasn't exactly the spot for a picnic. There was no running water and very little shade.

My dad consulted his watch. "It's a quarter till twelve. Shall we eat our lunch now, or would you rather look around a bit first?"

"Let's eat now, and I can look afterward." When I really started to look for the arrow marker I wouldn't want to stop for lunch. My father knew, of course, that I was searching for some clue to the lost Indian mine. If he thought it was silly or far out, he didn't say so. He was perfectly willing to humor me.

Rocky Meadows was a barren stretch of ground except for the rocks and a sprinkling of stunted pine trees. It would be hard to hide from anyone bent on spying. But the sky was free of Hank and his helicopter. Yet the Devil's Brow towered above the Meadows. A person with a good pair of binoculars could certainly spot us from there. It was a silly thought, and I put it aside.

When we had finished our lunch, Dad gathered up all of the sandwich wrappers and toothpicks from the deviled eggs and returned them to his knapsack. It was also his litterbag. Then he took out his notebook and pencils.

"If you intend doing any prospecting, get busy," he said. "I've a sermon to work on."

Some standing rocks had caught my eye, and I moved in that direction. All that I really knew was that somewhere on Gold Mountain there was supposed to be an arrow carved on a flat rock, and that the arrow marker pointed towards three large standing rocks. Between two of these rocks was supposed to be the entrance to a treasure cave or mine.

I passed different rock formations. Some were rocks on end. There were leaning rocks and rocks flat like fallen idols. There were rocks that formed caves and crevices. When I peered into some of these dark openings, I shivered. It would take a brave person to enter one of these caverns alone. Without the arrow marker you would be searching blindly. I began to appreciate the value of the arrow on the rock.

As I moved towards the rock cliffs that stretched upward

from the Meadow and formed the Devil's Brow, my footsteps slowed. The huge rocks that made up the main portion of the Brow seemed to be leaning outward. At intervals there were gaps where large boulders had become detached from the others making up the Brow and gone crashing down the mountain. Some of these had landed on the Meadows. Others had traveled on down the mountainside, carrying rocks and trees with them. Apparently when the devil frowned it was no small matter. I decided to do my looking in a safer spot.

But first I had to sit down. My knees felt suddenly weak. There was something about the place that was frightening. It's that old irrational fear again, I told myself. What was there to be afraid of? But those old feelings of fear were there, right in the pit of my stomach. I felt like I was getting ready to come face to face with something horrible and dreadful. It was right behind me, ready to spring. No, no, I told myself. This is no time to be afraid. What could possibly be out there—besides, my father is only a few feet away. Calm down, I told myself. But I felt the eyes watching me, and several times I thought I heard footsteps and a dog panting.

I forced myself to remain seated on the flat rock and at least regain some control before looking for the arrow on the rock. While seated on the rock, I had been nervously pulling moss from the top of the rock with my fingers and poking my finger in a groove. As I pulled more moss off the rock, the groove grew longer. With a shock I realized that my finger was actually being guided into a line—like an arrow.

It was several minutes before I pulled all the moss and tangle from around the rock—and there it was! Weathered and worn, but still distinguishable was an arrow with a broken shaft. It had been chiseled into the top of the rock. How long ago, there was no way of telling.

I heard my father calling: "Dawn! Time to be heading back—Dawn!" But I just sat there stunned. His booming voice came to me clearly, but it had no meaning.

Somehow I knew that the script was all wrong. It was Joe or Vicki who should have found the arrow. It was rightfully theirs. Somehow it was up to me to right the wrong. But at the moment there was something I must do. It was this thought that finally moved me.

The arrow marker was supposed to point towards three

upended rocks. I followed the line of direction and found that it really did. The three standing rocks formed a portion of the cliff that soared upward ending in the Devil's Brow. And between two of the rocks was an opening, hidden behind other rocks and hanging vines. Even the dwarfed pine tree was there. It was true to the sketch left behind by my friends' father.

The entrance looked dark and scary. Again I had the creepy sensation of being watched. I whirled about and scared a chipmunk. There was no other living creature in sight.

"Dawn! Can you hear me?—Dawn!" My father sounded closer. I could hear him crunching stones under his large shoes.

Frantically I tried to photograph the scene for my mental storehouse. But I couldn't seem to get any clear images. Many rocks seemed to be flat and long. Most of the standing rocks seemed to be in threes and have dwarfed pine trees growing from a crevice. I thought I could find the spot again but I wasn't sure.

I dug into the pocket of my lime-colored jacket and drew out the button that had popped off of Mother's jacket during the church service. I dropped the button at the foot of the flat rock that contained the arrow marker. Then I ran to meet Dad.

Dad looked at me closely when I rejoined him. I must have looked mixed up and confused. I was.

"Want to ride piggyback, if you're too tired?" Dad teased.

"Oh, Daddy!"

We started walking back. I thought about it for a long, long time, but I had to tell Dad about the arrow on the rock. I knew I could confide in him.

When I started telling him, it just all came out. I told him about Professor Greene's work, and how he had found something but died before he could get it all settled, about Hank and Nero, and about Vicki and Joe, and just everything.

"And I found the arrow back there, Dad. I honestly found the arrow, so that means that Joe and Vicki's dad was on to something.

"I'm familiar with Professor Greene's work. I remember reading about his theory about an advanced Indian culture in this area. That discovery could mean a giant step in archaeological studies in the area of Indian culture. I'd hate to see it ruined by someone who didn't realize what they were doing. The gold artifacts have monetary value, but that's not the real value. Their worth is in what they can tell us about people—a people who lived here a long time ago."

Dad seemed deep in thought. I was thinking too. It just didn't seem fair to me that I should find the arrow on the rock. It should have been Joe or Vicki who found the arrow, not me. "Dad, what am I going to do?"

"The first thing I want you to do is promise me you won't go inside that cave."

"Does that mean you don't want us to come here to search for the treasure cave?"

"I know how important it is to your friends to find the cave and help prove their father's theory, but if Hank is looking for it too, it could get dangerous. He won't try anything out in the open, but inside the cave could be dangerous. Promise me you won't go inside that cave."

"Promise," I answered. "Now, my problem is setting it up, so Vicki and Joe find the arrow for themselves."

"Just remember what I said."

"I will."

Later that night, after we had finished our evening meal, the rest of the family sat around the fireplace, but I went directly to bed. I was tired, but I think the main reason was to keep my brother or my mother from picking my brain.

I felt cold and got out of bed and put on my rose-colored pullover sweater. When I finally went to sleep, my dreams were of flat rocks that had arms and legs and hideously grinning faces. They kept jumping about and daring me to catch them. All of them seemed to have arrows sticking out of their backs.

About midnight my father woke me from my nightmares and told me that our cabin was on fire.

Chapter Seven

The fire had started with the shingles on the roof, and it was hot enough while it lasted. The local fire department put it out before it could do any real damage. It made all of our things smell of smoke for awhile, but that was about all. The pine-shingled roof wasn't so lucky. It was a mess.

Mother went about handing out coats and sweaters for us to put on over our pajamas, so we wouldn't catch cold. My father had already moved the station wagon out of danger and was loading it with our best clothing.

"How did the fire start, Doctor Carson?" the fire captain asked my father.

My father paused with an armload of clothing. "I don't rightly know. We had a small fire in the fireplace earlier in the evening. I was awakened about midnight by the smell of smoke. It was fortunate that you spotted it from the village."

"It started with a faulty chimney," my mother said with conviction. She slapped some smoky bath towels on top of the load Dad was carrying. "I've been at my husband to look at the flue, but he was afraid of disturbing some nesting birds."

"The nesting season is just about over." The fire captain masked a grin behind his hand. "And if it wasn't, it would be after you lit a fire in the fireplace." He became more serious. "We haven't had a normal rainfall, and everything is on the dry side. A spark from the chimney might have done it, if it happened to light on some dry pine needles or a pine shingle with a pitch pocket. Your cabin hasn't been occupied for a couple of seasons, and it should have been inspected."

"The man at the rental agency assured us that everything was in tip-top condition," Mother said firmly.

"Well, the insurance should cover any loss. If—" The fire captain was interrupted by one of his men touching him on the arm.

"Excuse me, sir," the fireman said, "but we found this on the roof. It was sticking into one of the shingles." He held up a portion of the shaft of a fire-blackened arrow.

The fire captain examined it. Looks like somebody's been playing Indian."

Father looked doubtful. He frowned at the captain over his armload of clothing. Why would anyone want to set fire to our cabin?"

"Who would do a thing like that?" Mother wondered.

"Some youngsters, likely," the fire captain said. "They probably thought it was just a prank. Lucky nobody got hurt." He turned to my father. "Sorry about this, Doctor Carson." Then he left to give some directions to his men.

Joe and Vicki jogged up. They had been awakened by the fire siren. Both had only taken time to pull on some clothes over their pajamas.

"When we saw it was your cabin we were petrified," Vicki told us.

Mother and Dad moved away to speak to some of our closer neighbors. I told Vicki and Joe about the arrow.

"I'd think it was Hank Woods," Vicki said, "if Joe and I lived in the cabin."

"Hank wouldn't want to scare any of us away until we found the treasure cave," Joe said. "He's planning on us leading him to it."

I felt a stab of guilt. Maybe this was the time to make a confession. But to tell Joe and his sister that I had discovered the arrow marker would spoil everything. It would take away the thrill that my friends would get from making the discovery for themselves—the excitement of following in the footsteps of their father.

"I say we were smoked by the Indian ghosts," Peter said.

"Why would they want to burn your cabin, silly?" Vicki asked. "We haven't found their treasure cave yet."

Once again I felt that stab of guilt.

"It was probably like the fire captain suggested," Joe said,

"—meant to be a prank. A prank that sure wasn't very funny."

"Joe! You forgot about the telegram!" Vicki exclaimed suddenly. "The one the agent gave you for their dad."

Joe slapped his pocket. "I sure did. It's for your father, and it may be important. I see him over there."

While the rest of us watched him anxiously, Dad opened the sealed envelope with his thumb. He read the message at least twice before raising his eyes from the paper.

"Well?" Mother was growing impatient.

"I have to go out of town for a few days," Dad announced calmly.

He took my mother's arm, and they walked away to talk privately. It wasn't unusual for Dad to be called away on business, so I didn't pay much attention to it. He'd be gone for a few days and back on Saturday in time to conduct service on Sunday.

My mother and father spent the rest of the night in the station wagon. Peter and I put our sleeping bags on our friends' porch. Vicki joined us, but Joe had to rise early. He slept with an alarm clock. Dad was gone before we woke up the next morning.

Peter and I helped move our things into a new cabin the rental agency found for us. To Mother's joy, the new cabin had a modern range.

Right after lunch, Vicki rode over on her bicycle and asked if Peter and I would like to go with her to the swim meet. It was the one Gloria had told us about. The meet was to be held in the Olympic-size swimming pool that belonged to the big hotel at Marble Mountain. It wasn't actually at Marble Mountain, but it was closer to Marble Mountain than it was to Gold Mountain. We could rent bicycles in the village. Joe wouldn't be able to go because he was working.

I wasn't exactly thrilled at the idea, but I could see that Vicki and Peter wanted to go, so I said yes.

Gloria was the big star, and Vicki had prepared me for that. But she was a lonely star.

After Gloria had splashed to an easy victory in the 100 meter freestyle there was only a faint spattering of applause.

"The other kids are jealous," Vicki told me. "They think she wins just because of her father's money. Gloria takes more swimming and diving lessons than all the others put together."

"Too bad he isn't here to see the results," I said. "Her father, I mean."

"Cal Benson is too busy making more money," Vicki said.

Actually it had been hard for me to concentrate on the swimming or diving. Although I did watch the events that Gloria participated in. I was still in a state of shock from the events of the past twenty-four hours.

First I had stumbled onto the arrow marker, the arrow on the rock. Then, while I was still numb from that, our cabin had been set afire during the night. Was the arrow that fired our cabin roof the result of a prank? Or was it meant to be a grim warning? Did someone know that I had discovered the treasure cave? How was that possible? These were some of the unanswered questions bothering me.

Luckily my brother was keeping Vicki busy with his own questions.

"If Benson is so rich, why doesn't he hire some rooters for Gloria, like they do on TV?" Peter asked.

"Maybe because he's never around long enough to see that she isn't that popular. It's a shame, because Gloria is really A-OK under her shell."

I heard their voices, but they seemed distant, far away. Perhaps it would be best for me to forget that I had ever seen the flat rock with its chiseled arrow marker. But I knew that was impossible. Peter and I had a date to hike to Rocky Meadows with Joe and Vicki the following Sunday. I had no intention of breaking that date.

Chapter Eight

The days dragged by. Joe was busy at the market, and Peter was entertaining Vicki. So I returned to my books. Reading had been my hobby for years—nothing to be afraid about. Gold Mountain did have a small library, but, oddly enough, I hadn't used it all summer. Funny, I was *doing* many of the things I'd read about in books. How could mere fiction compare to what I'd been doing?

It was just after making my first visit to the library that I had an experience that would have frightened the boots off the bravest 49'er. But, I handled it. It was the confrontation I had been dreading most. And yet it had an unusual, almost comical ending. There, blocking my path was Hank Woods and his dog, Nero.

My pounding heart choked me, and I was unable to move and scarcely to breathe as Hank and Nero came towards me. Hank was wearing sports clothes and had been exercising his dog. Nero was panting. Just as soon as I was able to get my heart out of my mouth I was going to scream.

"Glad I caught you," Hank said. He gave me what was probably meant to be a smile, but to my glazed eyeballs looked more like a leer.

It was Nero's behavior that made it a little easier for me to breathe. Nero was wagging his tail.

"I want to apologize for my actions on the trail the other day. I just got a little carried away. You can tell Joe Greene and his sister that it won't happen again."

I could only bob my head like a dummy. I guess my mouth was hanging as open as the Grand Canyon.

"Nero wants to apologize too. Shake hands with the young lady, Nero," Hank told his dog.

Immediately Nero sat on his haunches and extended his right paw.

I forced myself to take the extended paw. At any moment I expected Nero to change his mood and become a snarling killer. But it didn't happen. Even so, it was more frightening to me that a man could have such complete mastery over an animal. After a little while I dropped Nero's paw.

"I've been away for a few days," Hank told me. "I understand Doctor Carson is also away on business."

Joe was right. There were no secrets on Gold Mountain.

"How long will your father be away?"

I decided to be cautious. This was a *real* danger. Dad had told me that Hank could be dangerous. "Oh, he'll be home anytime now," I answered offhandedly, trying not to show how frightened I still was. Why was Hank being so nice? Just then the sheriff's patrol car cruised by. Hank seemed to get uneasy; he called Nero to "heel" and quickly moved on down the street.

I almost ran to Vicki's house. I could hardly wait to tell her about my strange, scarcely believable encounter with Hank Woods and his dog.

Vicki was scornfully skeptical. "Hank ought to win an Oscar for that act. He's up to something. You took your life in your hands shaking Nero's paw. I would sooner shake hands with a crocodile." She added: "Did he say anything about giving back the golden panther?"

I admitted that he hadn't mentioned the panther.

"When he returns Dad's artifact, I'll come nearer believing in his reformation," Vicki said.

In spite of Vicki's doubts, I felt a vast sense of relief. It would be a lot more fun leading Joe and Vicki to the arrow marker without the threat of Hank and his dog lurking in the background. Maybe the threat hadn't been entirely removed, but neither Hank nor his dog seemed quite as terrifying.

Joe was a bit skeptical of Hank's reformation, too, but not quite as openly as Vicki. "It doesn't sound much like the Hank I know," he said, when I told him about my meeting with Hank and Nero. "But I'm glad it turned out to be such a tame affair." He sounded a little like my father when he added. "We'll just have to wait and see if Hank's up to any tricks."

The next evening Peter and I went to our friends' house to plot some strategy and to plan for the coming hike.

"A couple of kids have confessed that they used a bow and some arrows to set fire to your cabin," Joe told us. "They said a man paid them to do it—a man with a beard."

"Hank has a beard," Vicki said.

"So do fifty other men in the area," Joe told her. "Hank wants us to lead him to the mine. Why try to scare us off?"

"He told Dawn he was away for several days. Maybe he didn't want us looking around the Meadows while he was gone," Vicki said.

"Maybe Hank doesn't need us," Peter said. "Maybe your dad told his dad about the arrow when he showed him the golden panther. Or maybe his dad followed your dad and saw the arrow for himself."

"Hank's father was a crippled man," Joe said. "I don't think he could have followed Dad over the steep trail from Stony Point to the Meadows."

"Dad never would have told Zeke Woods about the arrow on the rock," Vicki said stoutly. "That was a family secret. But we've simply got to find it before Hank does!" She made her hands into tight fists, and her eyes flashed.

Joe laughed. "No use getting up tight over a million to one shot. The risk of Hank finding the lost treasure cave or mine without knowing about the arrow is just that—a million to one."

And yet I found it! I wanted to blurt it out. I bit my knuckles and kept quiet. Biting my knuckles was something I often did, but I hadn't done it in a long while.

Something else was bothering me. There was a question I had meant to ask, but it slipped my mind. I knew I would think of it later.

Sure enough on the way home from our friends' house it came to me. I wanted to know if Hank Woods and the Breedloves were related. There was something about Mrs. Breedlove that reminded me of Hank. The question didn't seem too important.

The rock concert scheduled for Saturday had been canceled. Two of the "Mountain Rogues" had come down with the flu. Oddly enough, my relief from impatience and nervous tension came from an unexpected source.

I had stopped by to see Vicki on my way home from the library, and I recognized Gloria's black horse tied to a tree in the yard. Gloria was just leaving.

"Hi!" she said. Then she saw the books in my arms and made a face. "Do you really read those? Are you a bookworm? I've never met a real live bookworm."

"You have now," I told her coldly.

Vicki's laugh eased the tension somewhat. "You two make a great act. You should go on TV."

"I didn't mean to get you on your high horse," Gloria told me with a shrug. "No—that's only half true. I did mean to get you on a horse, one of mine. How about riding with me this afternoon? Vicki can't."

"Go ahead," Vicki coaxed. "You'll have fun. Don't be afraid, because Gloria will pick out something gentle. And the best part is that it won't cost you a cent. Gloria's dad owns the stable."

"Sure, I'll just put it on my expense account," Gloria said drily.

I was still fighting the dread in my insides at the thought of riding a horse, when suddenly Gloria swung up into the saddle of the black.

"I'll bring a horse around to your cabin right after lunch," Gloria told me. She turned her horse and rode away.

I wanted to yell, *What am I going to do?* But, instead I asked casually, "What will I wear?"

"Wear jeans," Vicki told me. "Gloria usually does if she isn't trying to show off. She'll probably wear something out of this world just to impress you. But all the other kids stick to jeans. Nobody tries to keep up with Gloria."

Mother was glad that I was going horseback riding with Gloria Benson. "This place has done wonders for you," Mom said. "Maybe being around kids your own age has helped. Dawn, you're quite a young lady, and you're blossoming into a lovely young woman." Then she rumpled my hair playfully.

Mothers have a way of saying things that just make you feel good all over. The problem is, what do you say? I decided that a big hug was answer enough. It helped to ease some of the queasies that had settled in that old familiar spot in my stomach.

I was standing at the window when Gloria rode up on her

horse, Duchess. She was leading a dapple-gray and was wearing a blue corduroy riding habit with fancy white stitching. It was a relief to see she wasn't wearing the Spanish outfit.

Mother came to the door to see me mount the dapple-gray. She had a greeting for Gloria and a word of caution for me. "Be careful, Dawn—you aren't used to horses."

"You don't need to be used to horses to ride Pacemaker," Gloria assured my mother. "He's really more like a rocking horse than flesh and blood."

The strange part was that I really did have a grand afternoon. Gloria was good company. She was a lot like my brother, saying the first thing that came to her mind and then maybe regretting it later.

There were other riders on the bridle path. Some of them nodded a greeting, but none of them tried to join us. I was beginning to understand why Gloria was lonely. She kept most people at a distance with her sharp tongue. I felt a little sorry for her.

The horseback ride had been fun, but as we were parting in front of my cabin Gloria spoiled it all.

"Next time you go hiking with Vicki and Joe I'd like to go along," Gloria said casually. "Vicki says it is OK with her and Joe if it's OK with you and Peter."

What could I say? I said the only thing that I could under the circumstances. "We're hiking to Rocky Meadows tomorrow. Come along if you want to. The more the merrier."

It was trite, but I felt trite. With Gloria along it would be a lot harder to put my plan into action. My plan was to make it look as if Joe or his sister had really discovered the arrow on the rock. I was surprised that Vicki would trust Gloria. She still considered Hank Woods a threat in spite of the apology he had made to me. And Hank was employed by Gloria's father. But I thought I knew the answer. Vicki felt sorry for the "poor little rich girl." Felt sorry for her just as I had been on the verge of doing. But Vicki didn't know that I had already found the arrow marker. She probably thought there was little chance of us discovering it on our first hike to the Meadows.

I sighed as Gloria sped away, and I turned to enter our cabin. It was just another problem that I had to solve.

Dad came back home after supper. He came in, put down

his bag, and within minutes he was gone again. His trip must have been a good one, I thought. He seemed happy, but busy.

Chapter Nine

Dad held early service, and right afterwards we set out for the meadows. Cal Benson, the sheriff, Mrs. Greene, and my mother and father were standing together when we said good-bye. Dad pulled me aside. "Remember your promise, Dawn."

"I know, when we find the arrow, we're to come back. We aren't to go inside the cave. Right?"

"Right. Good luck."

The perfect morning had one flaw—Gloria. It was awkward having her along, for more reasons than one. She was an outsider as far as the search for the lost Indian treasure was concerned. Besides, five is an awkward number on a hike. If the trail is wide enough for two people to walk side by side what do you do with the odd person? He has to be a pigtail, and too often that was me.

It wasn't that Joe preferred Gloria's company to mine. His grimaces, the faces he made behind Gloria's back, told me just the opposite. But she was always slipping and sliding on the gravel and needed to be helped over bad places in the trail. Her shoes weren't right for hiking. They were too low and kept filling up with gravel. Vicki had been able to talk her out of wearing riding boots.

No one was wearing boots today. I had learned my lesson. A good pair of heavy-soled shoes beat boots on a mountain hike. Evidently Joe and Vicki agreed with me, but my brother still preferred his tennis shoes.

"Sorry to be such a drag," Gloria said as she slipped and clutched Joe's arm.

It looked phony to me. I had seen the way she handled that

black horse. And I had seen her at the swim meet. Of course her shoes were impossible. But that was her fault.

"Man—does she ever need glasses!" I heard Peter mutter. "And I don't mean sun glasses."

When we left Gold River and swung towards Indian Springs, there was no sign of Hank's helicopter in the sky. I thought it was a good omen. But Vicki pointed out that it was Sunday. Cal Benson's workmen wouldn't be blasting and chipping away at the Devil's Brow. For that reason there was no need of Hank to be flying Benson's helicopter.

"I wouldn't be surprised to meet Hank and his killer dog around any turn of the trail," Vicki said darkly.

There were plenty of other hikers on the trail. Most of them wouldn't go any farther than Indian Springs. It was the most popular picnic spot.

Joe was loaded down with his full pack, his pronged stick— and Gloria. He handed his stick to Vicki.

We didn't have nearly as much freedom with Gloria along. No one felt like talking about the arrow on the rock and our search for the treasure cave. And that made conversation difficult, because it was about all we were really thinking about. Everyone but Gloria.

After we reached Indian Springs we took a break. While Gloria shook gravel from her shoes, Joe sat down near me on a rock.

"Was it your idea or Vicki's?"

I knew what Joe was talking about. He meant who was responsible for asking Gloria to come with us on the hike.

Because I wanted to be fair I said, "We both invited Gloria. She is left out of things and feels lonely."

"I can understand that." It was about as close as Joe ever came to being critical. He was testing the rope that was tied to his pack. When he was satisfied, he said that we ought to "hit the trail."

Joe and Vicki had left their walkie-talkies at home. They would just be in the way, Joe thought.

Gloria had another way of slowing progress. She had brought her camera and wanted to snap pictures constantly, just about every time we came to a likely looking rock or an observation point—and that was rather often. We had left most of the other hikers at the Springs.

"Get in the picture with me," Gloria would say. But some one had to operate the shutter. That was usually Joe's job.

"I wouldn't be caught dead in a picture with her," I heard my brother tell Vicki.

"Shh!" Vicki warned. "She might hear you."

For my part I didn't want to be caught alive in my faded jeans and lime-colored jacket standing beside Gloria in her scarlet slacks, white turtle-necked sweater, and red shoes.

We were making such slow progress that I was afraid it would be past noon before we reached Rocky Meadows. It seemed to me that my father and I had traveled twice as fast.

At one turn of the trail there were a lot of white-barked quaking aspens. Their leaves trembled and flashed in the sunlight like tiny reflectors. Gloria decided the trees would be a good background for a picture.

While Joe was waiting for Gloria to get posed, he told me something about the trees. "They used to be called no account. An aspen seldom lives more than eighty years, catches all sorts of diseases, and only grows to be forty or fifty feet tall."

"Sounds like some people I know," I told him.

"Who's talking about me?" Gloria had decided not to have her picture taken with the scene-stealing aspens and had returned. Now she was eyeing me suspiciously.

Everyone laughed except Gloria. She didn't know what the joke was until we told her.

Gloria acted as if she didn't think the joke was very funny. "Does your lecture come with the tour to Rocky Meadows or is it extra?" she asked Joe.

I felt like slapping her, but Joe only laughed.

"It comes with the grand tour," Joe said. "But wait till you get my bill. I don't come cheap as a guide."

"I'll put it on my expense account," Gloria told him airily.

"Today the aspen is valued," Joe continued, just as if there had been no interruption. "The pulp of the aspen makes fine paper. The trees prevent soil erosion. When the pines and other trees are destroyed by fire the aspen takes over. It covers the ground with millions of saplings—holds things together till the other trees get started again."

"I'll remind my dad to buy a few aspen forests," Gloria said.

Finally we reached the meadows and I suddenly lost

interest in what Gloria said or did. I was remembering something that I had completely forgotten. I had forgotten about leaving Mother's button at the foot of the flat rock. It was the button that had popped off her jacket in church, and I had kept it for her in the pocket of my lime-green jacket. I had put it by the rock, so that it would be easier to find the rock again. But I knew that Vicki would recognize the button. If she saw it, she would know that I had visited the spot before and that I had already found the flat rock with the arrow marker. I must recover Mother's button before it was seen by anyone else. But how could I shake the other searchers without arousing their suspicion?

It looked as if we had the Meadows to ourselves. We decided to eat first and look later. Gloria had brought her camera but no lunch. She probably expected a restaurant.

"No sweat," Vicki told her. "We have enough sandwiches and potato chips for an army in Joe's backpack."

"And the potato chips should be very *fine* potato chips by now," Joe said with a grin. "The way I've been heaving that pack around."

I had Peter's lunch and mine in my shoulder bag. My brother had also insisted that I make room for his flashlight. I'm sure he expected to find the lost treasure and check it out in a few hours time.

I scarcely knew what I was eating. My only thought was of the moment that I must slip away and recover Mother's button before the others started to search for the arrow on the rock. That metal button would glisten in the sunlight.

"Shall we tell her?" Vicki asked suddenly around a bite of sandwich.

"Might as well," Joe said.

I nodded. Gloria was bound to find out about our search for the rock and its arrow marker in a few minutes anyway.

"Tell me what?" Gloria sounded suspicious. "Don't tell me I have halitosis? What's wrong with my breath?"

We laughed.

"Tell you about looking for a treasure cave or a gold mine," Vicki explained. "That's the real reason we hiked to Rocky Meadows. Don't tell us you haven't heard of the famous Lost Indian Mine?"

Gloria made an impatient gesture with her hands. "Sure—

plenty of times. But I thought it was just a fairy tale like Cinderella."

"Hank Woods doesn't think it's a fairy tale," Vicki said. "He thinks we know right where it is. That's why he follows us and spies on us from the helicopter."

"And that's why he stole Vicki and Joe's golden panther," Peter put in. "He thinks it came from the treasure cave."

Gloria pretended to throw up her hands in despair. "Whoa! I can't digest all that on top of pimento cheese and potato chips."

"All you need to know right now is what we're looking for," Joe told her.

"We're looking for an arrow cut in the surface of a flat rock," Vicki said.

"With a broken shaft," Peter reminded.

That's what you're looking for, I thought grimly. I'm looking for Mother's button.

Joe looked at his watch. "We've only got about an hour, so we'd better get started. Spread out but keep in hailing distance. If you find the arrow, yell."

There had been no opportunity for me to slip away from the others and try to locate the button before it was discovered by someone else. But if I was careful I might still be able to put my plan into action. My plan was to find the button, hide it, and then casually lead Joe or Vicki to the flat rock with the arrow marker. That was my plan. This was the zero hour. Would it work?

Chapter Ten

It had all looked so simple when I went over the plan in my mind. I would give my companions the slip and speed right to the rock with the arrow marker. When I had recovered the button, I would drift away. Then, from a safe distance, I would say casually, "Look at those rocks. Don't they seem interesting?" I would be pointing in the direction of the rock with the broken-shaft arrow carved on its surface. Everyone would head in that direction. Eventually Joe or Vicki would find the arrow marker.

That was how it had worked in my mind. But things were going differently. Vicki was sticking close to me, and Gloria wasn't far away. Peter had demanded his flashlight and then gone with Joe in a different direction. But we were all aiming for the large standing rocks that formed the base of the Devil's Brow.

Today nothing looked familiar to me. What a simple fool I had been to think I could go straight to the flat rock with the arrow marker on its face and Mother's button at its base. That first time had been a pure accident. The trail to Rocky Meadows ended near where we had eaten our lunches. The rest of the Meadow was a rocky slope tilting gradually upward till checked by the up-ended rocks, a part of the granite tower topped by the Brow.

"This is spooky!" Vicki exclaimed. We had reached the standing rocks, and she was peering into a dark cave-like opening between two of the boulders. She stepped back with a shudder. "Without Dad's sketch of the arrow on the rock we'd never know which cave to enter. Likely we'd all fall into a deep hole."

I was thinking the same thing. But bitterness and regret sharpened my thoughts. I jabbed myself with them, feeling helpless and discouraged. Any of my companions had as much chance of finding the flat rock with the arrow marker as I did. What if it were Gloria, or even Peter? That would certainly make hash of my plans.

At that very moment my brother let out a whoop. "Hey! I've found a mine that's already been found."

We converged upon him and my heart had almost ceased to beat. What did Peter mean—a mine that's already been found? Could he have discovered Mother's button?

When I saw the NO TRESPASSING sign, Joe was already starting to read it aloud: *"This mining claim has been located and filed upon by Henry T. Woods."*

"That's Hank!" Gloria exclaimed. She swung on Vicki wide-eyed. "Is this the mine you were looking for?"

Vicki was unable to speak. Tears welled up in her dark eyes.

"We will know in a minute," Joe said. I had never seen his expression as serious. He glanced about and spied the flat rock. As he walked slowly towards it, I longed to sink from sight beneath the ground.

If Hank Woods had located the treasure cave it had to be my fault. In some fashion he had been able to spy on us and followed Dad and me the day we hiked to Rocky Meadows. It must have been Hank's eyes that I had imagined were watching me. And it had to be Hank who had set our cabin roof afire. He probably hoped to scare us away from Gold Mountain, so he could have the mine for himself at least until he had been able to file his claim.

Joe stooped over the rock, and I saw that his finger was tracing the groove of the arrow. He straightened at last. "It's the arrow on the rock, all right." I knew that the disappointment in his voice and in his face was more for Vicki than for himself.

"I don't believe it!" Vicki burst out. She hurried to her brother's side. Even after she had run her finger along the carved shaft of the arrow she seemed unconvinced. "Hank didn't know about the arrow. And without the arrow he simply

couldn't have found the mine."

Joe just looked at his sister but didn't say anything.

Suddenly Vicki stooped and picked up something from a patch of bare ground beside the flat rock. I knew that she had discovered Mother's button.

"Dawn—how could one of your mother's buttons be up here?" She was staring at Mother's navy button in open-mouthed wonder.

"I put it there," I admitted unhappily. It was impossible for me to meet my friend's eyes.

"You! When—why?" Vicki sounded as if she couldn't believe her ears.

I tried to swallow the lump in my throat. "The day we were supposed to hike to Rocky Meadows, the day Joe couldn't get away from the market, I hiked up here with my father."

"You found the arrow and didn't tell us!" Peter sounded just as surprised as Vicki, but he sounded mad too. "Dad knows, too. And didn't tell me!"

I nodded.

"I stumbled on the arrow marker by accident. It didn't seem fair. I wanted you or Joe to find it." I forced my eyes to meet Vicki's. "I dropped Mother's button at the base of the rock to help me find it again. I've—" It was hard for me to go on. "I've made an awful mess of things." I wanted to cry but was too ashamed to even do that.

Vicki put her arms around me and kissed me. "It isn't your fault, it's Hank's."

"Somehow Hank was suspicious and followed you," Joe said. "That's the only explanation. A shortcut leads from Stony Point to Rocky Meadows. It's steep but a man can make it. That is probably the way my dad came that day when Zeke Woods drove him in his jeep."

"Hank got here ahead of you and hid. He saw you find the arrow marker and the entrance to the treasure cave," Vicki said. She gritted her teeth. "I'm so mad I could chew rocks."

"Hank and his helicopter passed over us just as my father and I were making the turn towards Indian Springs," I remembered. "But he seemed on his usual route. He didn't circle around or anything."

Joe nodded. "If Hank spotted you on the trail he had more than enough time to land the helicopter at the heliport behind the Brow, get to Stony Point, and then take the shortcut to beat you to the Meadows. But how did he guess that you weren't stopping at Indian Springs? Did you tell anyone where you and your dad were headed?"

"I bought a map from the lady at the general store. She did seem curious when I said Dad and I were hiking to Rocky Meadows. Wanted to know if Joe had given me a tip about the lost mine."

"Fanny Breedlove is Hank's aunt," Vicki told me grimly. "She probably told Hank. But he doesn't come to the store often."

"He did that day," I said unhappily. I was remembering the red sports car I had seen driving into the general store's parking lot as I started home.

"This clears up the big mystery of Hank's sudden turn-about," Joe said. "Why he was a different person when you met him and Nero in Gold Mountain. He told you he had been away. While he was away he filed on this claim. Since he had found the lost mine and filed a claim, he didn't have to try to scare us away any longer."

"Why don't we just pull down Hank's sign and put up our own?" That was Peter's thought. "Dawn got here first and left Mother's button as a marker."

"Afraid that wouldn't be enough to convince a jury." Joe was beginning to sound more relaxed, more like his old self. "Stop blaming yourself," Joe told me. "We aren't even sure there is anything of value in that hole. If it's a treasure cave, the treasure may have been removed long ago."

"But what if it's a mine—the legendary Lost Indian Mine?" I asked.

"Then Hank may have the upper hand," Joe admitted, "if he really filed a claim." He added quickly: "But it was always a treasure cave in my great-grandfather's story. And my dad wasn't interested in finding a gold mine. He was hoping to find artifacts."

"If it isn't a mine but a treasure cave filled with artifacts or other treasure, it would be treasure trove. Right?" I saw a thin thread of hope.

"Right," Joe agreed.

"And if it's treasure trove, Hanks' mining claim won't cover it. Am I right?"

"That's my thought, but I'm not a lawyer," Joe told me.

"If it isn't a mine, why did Hank file a mining claim?" This thought wasn't such a happy one.

"I doubt if Hank has any idea what he filed on," Joe said. "Hank has heard of the Lost Indian Mine. He has also seen or has Dad's golden panther. He probably thinks it came from the mine. Thinks that the gold was mined and the artifact cast right in the same place."

"Maybe it was," I said unhappily.

"And maybe it wasn't. Dad didn't think it was. My guess is, that this cave isn't a mine at all. If it were, prospectors would have found it years ago. But the ore formations were all on the other side of the mountain."

"Let's keep our cool. And speaking of cool—it has been raining on us for five minutes."

Gloria shook herself and then ducked as there was a loud peal of thunder. "Trespassing or not, I'm getting out of this rain." She made a dash for the cave entrance.

My brother was close on her heels. He swung his arms and yelled for us to follow.

"No," I yelled. "I promised Dad we wouldn't go inside the cave."

"Don't come, then," Gloria shouted back. "Stay out there and get wet."

"I can't stop you, Joe, and Vicki. You can go in if you want, but I made a promise to my father, and I can't go inside."

"We're just geting in out of the rain. Storms in the mountains can get pretty rough," Vicki said.

"Maybe we can get back before it gets too bad," Joe said. "But if the lightening gets bad enough, it's really more dangerous to be among all these trees."

"I can't go inside the cave," I repeated. "Pete!" He didn't answer. I called again. "Peter, you come out here this instant. We're going back."

Suddenly, a clap of thunder jarred the earth. Lightning flashed and struck a tree, sending it crashing off the cliff. I stood frozen in panic. I couldn't go back. The only place to go was inside the cave. *O God, I am frightened. Please help me not to be so afraid. Help me to do the best thing.*

Chapter Eleven

We huddled together inside the ragged cave, wet and miserable. Joe had taken from his backpack a flashlight that was much stronger than Peter's. My brother had started to explore the cavern on his own, and I was worried. I could see the faint circles of light made by his flashlight as he went farther and farther along the narrow passageway.

"I've been inside a few mines," Joe told us. He swung the beam of light from his flashlight up and down and around. "This doesn't look like any of them. No signs of any mining here. Of course this is just the start."

"My father isn't going to like Hank trying to find a gold mine on company time," Gloria said.

I was really getting worried about my brother by now. The faint circles of light that marked his progress were no longer showing. Either his battery had gone dead, or he had passed around a bend of the tunnel.

The interior of the cave looked dark and scary, but I moved slowly away from the others. I had to find Peter before he went too far.

"Wait!" Joe stopped me. "You can't see without a light. I'll check on Peter."

Joe's flashlight beam made the dark passageway look even more spooky. "Pete!" he called. "Pete—if you hear me, answer."

There was a short silence, and then my brother's voice rang out hollowly: "Down here—in this pit. I dropped my flashlight and had to go after it."

We followed Joe for about a hundred feet back into the cave. Just as the interior became so small that you could no longer stand without stooping, there was Peter. He was off the rocky shelf and only the top of his head showed. His hair looked orange in the beam of light that Joe turned on him.

When my brother climbed out of the pit and joined us, he was carrying his useless flashlight in one hand and a small object in the other.

"Light went out when it struck the rocks," Peter explained. "Battery was about shot anyway." Then he showed Joe the object he held in his hand. It looked like a small narrow rock. "Found this in a sort of hole in the wall."

Joe took the object and examined it. I thought it had a yellowish cast but that was probably due to the light from the flashlight. Joe kept looking at it and turning it over and over in his hands. Finally he rubbed it against another rock. The other rock formed part of the rough wall of the tunnel. Then he looked at it again.

"It's heavy enough to be a bullet," Peter said, "but it isn't the right shape."

"It's an artifact," Joe said. It sounded as if he was keeping his voice steady with an effort. "And it is made of gold."

No one spoke for a full minute. It was like a fairy tale. We had all been turned into statues.

"O boy!" Peter finally shattered the spell. He looked ready to dive back into the pit.

Joe restrained him. "We need to play this cool." He let each of us hold the small artifact in our hands.

It was a small object and looked as if it was meant to be some sort of a lizard. In the beam from Joe's flashlight it was hard to make out too much of the detail.

"Then Dad's golden panther did come from this treasure cave," Vicki said. She clapped her hands. "Dad's theory was right."

"There must be a lot more of them down there," Peter said. "We ought to get all we can carry."

"No," Joe said, "we better not disturb anything." He took the artifact from Vicki and handed it to Peter. "Put it back where you found it."

"In a pig's eye!" Peter sounded defiant.

Joe kept his cool. "Hank has filed a claim to this cave. He

already has the golden panther. If we show up with a gold lizard, he'll claim it came from his cave and belongs to him under the law of treasure trove. But if Hank doesn't know about the lizard and can't prove that the golden panther really came from his mine—Well, then we have a better chance of getting the panther back and claiming treasure trove ourselves. Anyway, we need the opinion of a lawyer before we disturb things."

"If it is treasure trove, maybe the Indians have a claim," I suggested.

"Ugh!" I could imagine Vicki making a face in the shadows.

"Possession is nine points of the law," Peter grumbled. But he went back down into the pit. The golden lizard was clutched tightly in his fist.

My brother had just rejoined us, when there was a menacing rumble. We had been too busy to think of the storm outside.

"Thunder bugs me," Gloria admitted as she cowered. So Gloria was scared of something, too.

The thunder grew into a roar that was louder than any thunder I could remember.

Joe had been listening with a serious expression on his face. He took a step towards the cave entrance and then swung about. "That isn't thunder—it's a rock slide!"

"I'm getting out of here!" Gloria cried. She made a dash for the entrance.

In the beam from Joe's flashlight I saw Gloria recoil and fall to the floor of the cave as tons of rock and debris closed the doorway. It was lucky for her that she had lost the race. But how lucky? She was one with the rest of us—buried alive.

Chapter Twelve

Joe brought Gloria back to be with the rest of us and then went to examine the blocked entrance. We waited in a fearful huddle. I found a hand and pressed it, and it returned my pressure. I thought the hand belonged to Vicki, but it might have been Gloria's. Peter's fingers dug into my other arm.

When Joe returned, he told us what we already suspected. Tons of rock had closed the passageway through which we had entered the treasure cave. At least that was the way it looked from this side. There wasn't a sliver of light from the outside world and all sound had been blocked out.

"It's up to us to find another exit," Joe told us firmly, "and we will."

"With God's help," I agreed in a low voice.

Naturally Joe took command. He was the oldest, and he had the only flashlight, our source of light. But he was also a natural leader. I knew now why my mother had said that he was more adult than most adults she knew.

Joe didn't give us time to be really scared. He kept us busy. Handing Vicki his flashlight to hold, he dug into his backpack.

It was really super—all that Joe had been able to crowd into that pack. He produced a fat candle and lit it with a match torn from a paper book of matches. Even the flickering little flame brought a ray of comfort.

"The candle will be yours, Dawn," he told me. "While it burns we'll know there is oxygen. If it goes out, be sure to let me know." He handed me the candle and the little match book.

The ground we had already been over was fairly level, so

Joe guided us back to the point where my brother had gone into the pit and found the gold artifact. He used his flashlight sparingly because he wanted to save his battery. Although he had a spare in his pack, he didn't want to waste any light.

When we reached this point, Joe made us get down on our hands and knees. The passage had begun to narrow. The beam from Joe's flashlight showed a scary path ahead—narrow rock ledges and dark pits or drop-off places.

"I'm going to tie us together with my rope," Joe explained. "Then, if anyone slips, the rest of us will be like an anchor."

I knew that Joe was thinking about the Indian who had lost his life in the treasure cave. He had fallen from one of these very same ledges, if you could believe the story told to Joe's great-grandfather by the old Indian. It was easy to picture someone falling from this ledge. I tried to blot the thought from my mind.

One end of the rope Joe knotted about my waist, and then he made a loop around Peter, Vicki, and Gloria. The reason that Gloria was next to Joe was that she was the one most liable to slip, he said. I was the last because I was heavier than either Peter or Vicki and guardian of the precious candle. It made sense, but I wasn't crazy about being last.

The pack Joe carried couldn't be left behind, because it contained too many things we might need, but he made Gloria give up her camera, and I had to jettison my shoulder bag.

We started our scary journey crawling along on our hands and knees. Our only light was the beam from Joe's flashlight. What we were able to see made it all the more frightening. It was better to inch along on the heels of the person ahead and look neither left nor right.

Joe made frequent stops to rest us and lend encouragement. "You can tell there has been water along here once. The side wall is worn and smooth. If you listen real hard you can hear water dripping somewhere," Joe told us.

"I thought it was just my wet clothes," Gloria said. It was an attempt to put a spark of lightness into a grim situation, but none of us could appreciate it at the time.

At the next stop Joe asked about the candle. "OK so far," I answered. Somehow I was getting a certain amount of comfort from nursing the tiny flame.

When Joe stopped again, he had brought us to the end of a

narrow shelf. There was a dropping-off place, he told us, and he wanted to do some investigating before going ahead. He untied the rope from about his body and stood up.

For some unknown reason Gloria decided to follow Joe's example. Maybe she felt cramped. As she stumbled to her feet she jerked the rope that bound her to Vicki and was thrown off balance. To save herself she grabbed Joe.

To keep from plunging off the ledge, Joe seized a rocky knob with both hands. He was forced to release his grip on the flashlight. It bounced off the rocks below, and there was a splash.

Gloria broke the deep silence that followed with a sob. "It's my fault—everything's my fault—my fault we entered the cave to get out of the rain—even the rock slide is my fault, or my father's."

"Today is Sunday," Joe reminded her. "Your father's men weren't setting off dynamite charges. Maybe the devil doesn't like dynamite. Maybe he doesn't like sun and wind and rain, either. The big rocks in the Brow have been puckering up for a long time, just waiting for a nudge. It won't be any easier to find our way out of here without a flashlight, but we'll make it."

"Maybe your spare battery would fit my flashlight," Peter suggested. Then I felt my brother give himself an impatient shake. "I left my flashlight back there when you made us strip down."

"It's OK," Joe said. "We did learn something. There's water down below. I aim to find out how much. The rest of you keep quiet and don't move around."

"You can't be spared," Peter said, "Besides, I'm smaller. It will be easier to lower me on the rope and pull me up again."

"It's dark down there," Joe reminded.

"I can carry Dawn's candle."

"OK, but don't take any chances. All I want to know is how deep is the water? Does it flow through an opening big enough for us to squeeze through?"

Joe untied the rope from around our bodies and fastened it under Peter's armpits. Then we all took hold of the other end and lowered my brother and his flickering candle into the pit. I had never been so proud of Peter in my whole life.

When we pulled Peter back up to the ledge, his report was negative. There was water, but it seemed to disappear into the ground. He couldn't see any opening at all. But the candle was not too much help. But when he tried to move around, he just ran into rock walls. It looked like a dead end.

My brother gave me back the candle, and it was like one tiny lightning bug trying to brighten a tomb.

I was afraid to cry for fear my tears would put out the fragile flame. The situation seemed hopeless. We couldn't go forward, and it was useless to retrace our steps. I began to pray silently but desperately.

Chapter Thirteen

Joe was not ready to surrender. He told Peter that he had done a good job of spying out the land. Then he made us all turn around. Afterwards he refastened the rope about our waists. It was a slow job, because all he had to work by was the tiny candle flame.

"What good is going back?" Vicki asked the question for all of us. Her voice sounded weary and defeated. And that was unusual for Vicki.

"We're only going a short ways," Joe told his sister. "There's another passageway to check out. I followed this one because it was the larger."

I told Joe to keep the candle but he said it would only be in his way. He was getting sort of used to being a mole. You had to feel your way and stay as close to the middle of the rock shelf as possible.

We inched along, and at last we came to the other opening. The hole seemed so small as it was revealed by my flickering candle, that I was afraid I would get stuck. But Joe had made it as well as the others, so I exhaled and squeezed through.

On the other side of the keyhole was a cave-like room with a ceiling that permitted us to stand erect. It was a wonderful sensation. But my relief turned to dismay when I saw that the candle flame had gone out.

"The candle went out!" I cried in alarm.

Joe laughed. "It was blown out. Feel that draft?"

Sure enough I could feel a current of cool fresh air. It seemed to be coming from a small opening in the ceiling,

although it was too dark to tell exactly.

It was hard to leave the big room and get down on our hands and knees again. Once again the tunnel narrowed. It turned and twisted and seemed to be diving into the very heart of the mountain. My relighted candle flickered weakly.

My despair returned and I prayed as I had never prayed before. If I ever got out of this alive I was going to be a different sort of a person. I would be a better sister to my brother and a far better daughter to my parents. I would even be a better mistress to my kitten, Sheba. And I would be less critical of Gloria Benson.

Gloria must have been having some trouble with her own conscience, because I heard her say in a muffled voice to Vicki, "I'm sorry I've been such a stupe."

"You're not a stupe," Vicki told her. "I'm glad you're with us. I mean—we're all in this together."

"When we get out of here—" I almost said "if," but caught myself in time. "When we get out of here, you're going to teach me to ride a horse," I told Gloria.

"And you're going to teach me to do a swan dive," Vicki said.

"When we get out of here, you can teach me everything—except about rocks," Gloria said. "I'll already know about them."

"Man!" my brother grunted. "This cave is a pushover. Someday Joe and I will show you a real one."

It was just talk to keep our spirits up, and we knew it, but it did seem to help.

Joe was too busy for talk. He checked us suddenly. "This shelf ends dead ahead, and I hear running water. Dawn, pass me your candle."

I passed along the candle, and when Joe waved it back and forth I fancied that I could see a shadowy movement in the deep pit below. It looked scary and gave me the creeps.

"Pete—ready for some more exploring?" Joe asked my brother.

"Sure."

Once again we lowered Peter into the unknown. The tiny flame of the candle he carried cast weird and eerie shadows as it painted the pit with patches of light. I held my breath.

I heard my brother enter the water, and a moment later he

gave a cry of triumph that rang hollowly in the cave. "I'm wading!" Then his dancing candle passed out of sight.

This time, when we pulled my brother back up to the rock shelf, he was excited. "The water runs right under a big rock and disappears. I don't know where it goes."

"Let's go see," Joe said.

When we had been lowered one by one into the dark pool of water and only Joe remained on the ledge, we wondered how he meant to join us. He ran the rope around a big rock—he told us later—and then made a loop for his foot. Playing out the rope little by little, he lowered himself. After he had joined us, he reclaimed the rope.

The rock tunnel did not seem as dark now. I thought at first it was because my eyes had grown accustomed to the darkness. But Joe pointed out the slits and cracks in the ceiling and upper walls. They acted as light wells and allowed ribbons of light to reach us. I never had realized that sunlight could look so beautiful.

We waded along the rocky bed of the spring, and the water felt cool but not actually cold.

Then just as I was allowing myself to feel a warmth of hope, icy disappointment struck again. We came to the large boulder that Peter had mentioned. At this point the spring seemed to end abruptly. A closer look showed that it was pulled down under the rock. There was a strong movement of the water as it was swept into the under-the-surface channel.

"It goes down under that big rock," Joe said. "But is there an opening big enough for us to get through? That's the one hundred and twenty-eight thousand dollar question. I'm going down to see." He slipped off his pack and started to unbutton his shirt.

"Stop!" Gloria faced him. She seemed excited, and her words came with a rush. "This is my turn—my ball game. I can swim and dive, if I can't do anything else. You can tie the rope around my waist. If I get through, I'll fasten it to a tree or around a rock. If I don't make it, you can reel me in."

Joe was doubtful, but Vicki sided with Gloria. "She's better in the water than you are," she told her brother.

I had never seen Joe in the water, but I thought that his sister was probably right. I had seen Gloria in the hotel pool.

Gloria had already started to undress. "Don't worry, I'm

wearing my bathing suit. I was dumb enough to plan taking a dip at Indian Springs."

As I watched Gloria disappear into the black water under the big rock, I was thinking: How wrong can you be about a person?

Joe kept playing out the rope, and the rest of us held our breath and kept our fingers crossed. She was either making an extra deep dive or else she had made it to the outside.

Suddenly the rope that Joe had been playing out became taunt. Joe looked at us but he didn't say anything.

We shouted our relief when Gloria's dripping head reappeared. Joe pulled her up beside us, and her teeth were chattering.

"It's colder than you think—down deep." She was stretching it out like a TV master of ceremonies on an award show, making us wait for the big news. But it was OK, because we knew she had made it to freedom.

"There's a hole under that rock big enough for Dawn's father to swim through," Gloria told us when she had regained her breath and decided that she had kept us waiting long enough. "I tied the end of the rope to a pine tree. And did I hate to return to purgatory! I almost didn't," she added with an impish and a very wet grin.

It was mostly easy going after that. Joe made the other end of the rope secure around a handy boulder inside our rock prison. Then one by one we followed the guide line to safety and freedom. We just let our hands slide along the rope as the current pulled us down and through the underwater channel.

The underwater spring was the source, or one of the sources, of Gold River. It poured out from under the big rock in a thicket of scrub pines and was speeded on to a meeting with Snow Creek by a small waterfall. After the two streams had merged, it became the familiar Gold River.

Joe was the last to make the underwater journey to freedom. When he scrambled out of the water, we gave him a big cheer. He certainly did deserve one. As you might guess, he was towing his backpack.

"Thank God we're out of there," Joe said. He was just now beginning to show the strain he had been under.

I had already offered up a prayer of thanks. It was a silent prayer, but it came from my heart.

Joe had brought Gloria's rolled-up clothing in his pack. She made a face as she started to put on the soggy garments.

"I have only one regret," Joe said. He sounded wistful. "I wish I had told Peter to keep the gold lizard. It would have meant a lot to Mother, knowing Dad was right in his theory about the ancient Indians."

I was looking at my brother, and I saw he had a strange expression as Joe was speaking. With a hitching movement he dug into his pocket and produced the tiny artifact.

"Here," Peter said, offering the gold lizard to Joe. "I just couldn't make myself part with the little fellow. I didn't want Hank to get him, but you can have him."

"You found it." Joe said. "Under the law of treasure trove—"

"Your dad is the one who really found it," I said. "Without the arrow on the rock we wouldn't have found the cave. Besides, what possible use could Peter have for a gold lizard?"

Peter gave me a strange look. But for once he was willing to have me speak for both of us. "Dawn's right," my brother agreed. "I belong to the Beaver Patrol."

Chapter Fourteen

Suddenly we heard voices, lots of voices. Then we heard the calls. "Dawn!" "Peter!" That was my dad's voice. "Joe! Vicki!" That was Mrs. Greene's voice. "Gloria!" That was Mr. Benson's voice.

Excitedly we answered and ran towards the voices. I reached Dad first. I was so excited that the words started tumbling out one on top of the other. Then I noticed I wasn't the only one talking. Peter was chattering. Gloria was telling her version of what had happened. Joe and Vicki were telling their mother about the cave and how it meant that their father had been right. We sounded like a bunch of turkeys.

"Let's get you kids home before you all catch pneumonia," my father said.

It was exciting being taken off the slopes by helicopter but it wasn't until later, when we all gathered at our cabin, that we finally realized how dangerous our situation had been. All the pieces began to come together.

Dad explained: "I was in Washington last week," he said. "I talked to some people at the Smithsonian Institute. They're sending a team out to look at the cave. If it is what Professor Greene thought, then there is indeed a treasure. It isn't a gold mine, but probably one of the most notable archaeological finds of the century. You should be very proud of your father's work."

Joe was beaming as he hugged his mother. He had never really wanted a gold mine. He just wanted to prove his father's work had not been in vain.

"What about Hank's claim?" Vicki asked.

"It doesn't count," Dad said. "He filed on a gold mine. There is no gold mine."

"Besides," added Cal Benson, "I own the mountain. He couldn't file on that claim without my permission. I have an idea Hank was planning to use Gloria in some way to force me into going along with his plan."

"Kidnapping?" I asked.

"Possibly, but I was warned by Pastor Carson in time, and I'm grateful to him." Gloria snuggled against her father. She looked happy, for she had learned that she had an inner wealth of courage. She didn't need to rely on her father's money to make friends.

Cal Benson continued. "When Pastor Carson came to see me the evening Dawn found the arrow on the rock, I put in a few calls to Washington. Things started happening fast."

Mrs. Greene spoke up next. "I couldn't believe it when Cal came to see me that evening with the news. All those years I'd wanted to believe in my husband's work, but it all seemed like a fairy tale, something kids believe in. Then to learn that it was possibly true—well, I couldn't believe it. I still can't. It's too wonderful. I spent most of the night going through my husband's papers and notes to have ready for Pastor Carson to take to Washington the next day."

"I didn't tell you kids, because I didn't want you to get excited and then have another letdown. Besides, Cal had told me about Hank. Hank had followed us the day we hiked to the Meadows," Dad said to me. "He saw you find the arrow on the rock."

"Just as I suspected," said Joe.

"The fire had me worried," Mother said. "I knew that Hank fella had to be pretty desperate. Your father didn't want to go, but I convinced him to go."

"I was sure Hank had something to do with the fire, so I called the sheriff, and he's had you kids and Hank under a constant watch," Cal Benson said. "I confronted Hank with his treachery, then fired him, but not before I got something back that belongs to the Greene family." He took the golden panther and gave it to Mrs. Greene.

Dad continued: "When you kids went out today looking for the arrow on the rock, we were going to join you and give you the good news. But the storm came up, and we were delayed. I knew you'd probably go inside the cave for shelter. I had no more fear about Hank; he was long gone, but I *was* worried about the rock slides.

"I'm sorry," I said. "We had no other choice, but to go inside."

"I understand, but do you see why I was concerned? When we saw that the rock slide had covered the cave entrance, we were sure we'd never reach you in time. It was a miracle that you were able to find another way out. I thank God for that!"

We all told how Joe had kept his head and led us out safely. Joe turned to me. "If Dawn hadn't been so calm, I don't think I could have made it. She gave me an example. I was scared to death, but—Dawn you were just super!"

Me? I didn't know what to say. Chicken me, being an example for anybody! Dad smiled. We both knew what a long way I had come.

As a reward for his major role in leading us out of our rock prison, Gloria's father gave Joe a new job. Joe was put in charge of laying out a nature walk for guests at Benson's big hotel on the road to Marble Mountain. "You can choose your own staff of helpers," Cal Benson said.

Joe looked around the room. "Oh, I don't know. Maybe I'll put an ad in the paper and see what happens."

"You'll do what?" Vicki said. "You've got the best trail-blazers in the world right here, and—"

"OK, OK! You convinced me." We were all recruited right there on the spot. The trail will have markers at various points of interest. Trees and flowers will be identified.

"Does that offer include me?" Gloria asked shyly.

"You bet," Joe said.

Gloria laughed. "Just think, I'll be on your payroll, Dad." Her father smiled and then suggested that they go home. As they said good-bye, I knew that it would not be the last time they visited our cabin. He liked Dad, and Dad liked him.

When the others said good-bye for the evening, Mom hugged Mrs. Greene, and I knew they were going to be friends, just like Joe and Vicki were our friends. Vicki turned to us, her face was beaming. Her happiness came out in a burst of emotion. "The arrow on the rock really did point to treasure. Searching for it brought me close to three priceless friends."

That night I said my prayers. Safe and warm beneath the covers, I thought about the events of the past few weeks. My brother was learning that caution isn't the same as fear. Good judgment isn't the same as being frightened. There is a difference. He was learning it—and so was I.

I had stopped asking God why I was afraid. Now I was asking Him to help me exercise good judgment and caution in a difficult situation. So far it is working—with just an occasional attack of the queasies.

Chapter One

It was the day before Christmas. Stacy Benton was admiring the decorated tree in the alcove of the bay window. Usually her mother's piano stood there, but during the holidays it was moved to the side wall. Stacy walked over to the wide, fieldstone fireplace and straightened the box of matches on the mantel. Next, she fingered the bayberry candle that stuck up through the holly arrangement on the coffee table.

How she loved Christmas!

Suddenly the phone rang. She grabbed the receiver on the second ring.

"Hello. Oh, hi, Barb. What's up?"

Barb Anderson, tall, dark-haired and dark-eyed, was one of four classmates she traveled around with at school. Stacy felt that if anyone asked who her best friend was, she'd surely say Barb.

"Are you still going with us to Beaver Creek?" Barb asked.

"Oh, sure."

Between Christmas and New Year's, Barb and her parents—she was an only child—were going to a Colorado resort for a week of skiing. They had invited Stacy along. At last she was going to learn to ski. When she had told her mother about it two weeks ago, her mother didn't actually say OK, but she didn't have to. Why would Mom say no?

"I can't wait," Stacy said now. "How about you?"

"Same here," Barb answered. "Well, we're in the middle of decorating the tree, so I have to go. See you."

Excited and happy, Stacy picked up a gingerbread man from the plate of cookies on the coffee table and bit the head off.

Mom still made them for her and Giles, even though she was almost 13 and Giles was 15.

To make everything more wonderful, it was snowing. She glanced through the window at the soft white mounds forming on the evergreens outside.

Just then Mom came in with a handful of cards. "Here, run down to the post office, please, for some stamps and mail these."

Stacy slipped into her sheepskin-lined jacket. "Sure, but where's Giles?" She wasn't going to argue about her brother going to the post office instead of her as she usually did. Not today. She welcomed the excuse to walk in the snow.

"Oh, over at the new mall," Mom answered with a soft smile. "A little last-minute shopping, I guess."

Stacy tied a scarf over her straight, chestnut hair. Maybe she'd put some curlers in it tonight, so the ends would be turned up for Christmas. She and Giles had the same amber-brown eyes, but why did he have to have the blond curly hair? She looked like Dad and Giles looked like Mom. It should have been the other way around. Oh, well, she was too happy to care about that now.

Taking the cards Mom handed to her, she giggled. "It's silly to mail cards the day before Christmas."

"Well, we received some from these folks today, and I want to send them one," Mom said, "At least they'll be mailed before Christmas. And hurry, so you'll be home before dark."

Stacy laughed again. She had felt good all day, but Barb's call had made her bubbly-happy.

"Who was on the phone?" Mom asked at the door.

"Oh, Barb. She just wanted to make sure I was going on the skiing trip with them."

"But, Stacy," Mom began. She looked sort of upset. "I didn't say yes. I said Dad and I would talk it over."

"Oh, Mom," Stacy teased. "You always say yes in the end. I know you." She planted a quick kiss on Mom's cheek and ran down the front steps.

She was passing the third home down the street, when she heard a grating sound. It was a little red-haired boy named Rusty. He was about five and always rather pale. Now he was trying to coast in the thin layer of snow on his walk.

"Hi, Stacy," he called.

"Hi, Rusty, how many Easter eggs are you going to get for Christmas?"

Rusty laughed. It was their little joke. She would always ask him if he got things connected with another special day.

"You don't get Easter eggs. You get presents, dummy."

There was genuine fondness in the way he called her "dummy." Then he laughed again. He never seemed to play with other children. And he seemed hungry for friendship. Maybe after he started school he'd find some little pals.

Stacy walked on, reveling in the snowfall. Bushes and trees were all coated. Only here and there points of grass still stuck through the sparkling whiteness. After she left the post office, she dawdled in front of Leckerman's Department Store, looking at the outfit on the mannequin in the window. It was a purple-plaid pleated skirt—she loved purple—a lavender suede vest and a white blouse. She had plenty of white tops, but she had put the skirt and vest on her Christmas list.

Her list also included the latest album by Deep Ocean, a rock group, and last but most important, skis and ski clothes.

The storefronts were decorated. So were the lampposts and a huge tree in the square. At dusk they would be all lit up. She wished she could wait to see them, but that would be too late. As she headed for home, she scooted her feet along the sidewalk making long, slithery tracks in the snow. Golly, life was good.

Going along, she daydreamed as usual. Maybe—someday—she would be famous. Maybe on the stage. No, she grinned, remembering the school play last year. She was no good at memorizing lines. But the teacher told her she had a strong, clear singing voice. Maybe—someday—she would make her own albums. And she would sign her full name across the cover—Anastasia Virginia Benton. It would look impressive. She liked her full name, but right now she liked Stacy much better. And who cared about being famous? She had all she wanted up to now. Why change? Let life go on the same.

At home she found that Dad and Giles had come in. Dad was slouched in a fireplace chair, staring at the tree. He was a tall, broad-shouldered, muscular man.

Giles, sitting opposite him, hunched forward. "I saw in a magazine at the library about this new kind of business," he told Dad. "It doesn't take long to get started, and you can make five hundred dollars—"

3

"Giles, stop being so money-minded," Dad said. "Too many people get cheated by such ads."

All Giles thinks about is money, Stacy thought, grinning. Then she called, "Hi, guys."

Dad nodded. "Hi, Stacy."

Giles looked up at her. "Want to go caroling tonight? Anne said I should ask you."

"Sure, why not." She didn't belong to a choir or any singing group, so she hadn't thought about it before. One time the organist in church was recruiting members for a junior choir. When Stacy mentioned it at school, Barb and some of the other girls thought it was corny. "You'll have to practice a lot," one had said, "and it will get in the way of other things." Stacy had let them sway her decision. She didn't want to give up her friends.

"Anne couldn't get many," Giles went on. "Everyone has something else to do."

Anne was a friend and classmate of his even though she was a year older. She had her own car, too.

Humph, Stacy thought, if Anne had a big enough group, I wouldn't have been asked. Oh, well, why be touchy about it. Caroling would be fun.

"OK, I'll go."

She ran upstairs and, lying across her bed, she just looked around her pink and white room with the fluffy purple rug and purple cushions. She had her own TV set there in the corner. Beside it stood her own phone and a record and tape-player. She had a full bookcase, although she took little time to read anything except schoolbooks. She had a closet full of clothes and a generous allowance every week.

The only things she wanted now were the skis, a ski outfit, and the plaid skirt and vest. And she'd get them for Christmas. She wondered where Mom had hidden them. Mom changed the hiding place every year, so that she and Giles couldn't find the gifts ahead of time.

A short while later, she heard Giles shouting up the stairs that it was time to eat.

All through supper, Stacy sensed a strained feeling. But it must be her imagination, she told herself. Mom was tired from the Christmas preparations, and Dad probably was preoccupied with all the bowl games he'd watch during the holidays.

He liked football. Or maybe, they just didn't feel like talking much.

Giles didn't seem affected, though. He glanced at the wall clock and put his napkin on his plate. "Mmm, going on seven. Anne should be here soon."

"How long will we be gone?" Stacy asked him.

"Till about nine-thirty."

"Good," Stacy said. "We'll be home in plenty of time to open our gifts." That had been their Christmas Eve custom for many years.

Giles only shrugged, but Mom and Dad looked at each other. Then they rose from the table.

Stacking the dishes hurriedly, Mom cleared her throat. Then she said, "About your gifts—you won't be getting all you asked for this year." She kept her eyes on the plates she was putting on top of each other. Dad remained silent.

"Why?" Stacy asked with a rather shocked feeling crawling over her.

Just then the beep of a horn out front told them that Anne had come for them.

"What do you mean, Mom?" Stacy asked again. All she could think of were her skis.

"Come on," Giles cut in, tossing her jacket to her. Half into his own coat, he dashed out.

Stacy gave Mom a wondering look and followed him.

"Have a good time," Dad called to them as she was closing the door.

But how could she enjoy the caroling now, after what Mom had said about their gifts? And why? Remembering all the other years when she and Giles received everything they asked for, why would Mom say a thing like that?

Chapter Two

Anne picked up another boy and girl, and her own sister and brother went along. That made seven of them, all high school kids except Stacy.

The moon shone brightly, giving the snow a bluish tinge. Tree lights twinkled in windows, and wreaths hung on front doors.

They went down Larkin Street from First to Second to Third Avenue. At each stop they sang one or two of their favorites: "Silent Night," "O Little Town of Bethlehem," "The First Noel," and "Oh, Come All Ye Faithful."

Stacy loved all the carols, but tonight her heart wasn't in singing. She slurred over the words and mumbled in places.

"Come on, Stacy," Anne urged at one time. "You have a good, clear voice. Sing louder." Then she laughed slightly. "We have to make up for the ones who aren't here."

Stacy felt like a little kid being talked down to by a grown-up. But she tried, and her voice rose higher and stronger. She was glad, though, when they called it a night and walked back to the car.

"Now," Anne said, "we're going back to my place for some refreshments."

Even that couldn't raise Stacy's spirits. Would she get her skis? The thought made her so uneasy, she scarcely tasted the brownies and soda pop.

Giles, as usual, was enjoying himself. He struck up a conversation with the other boy. "Gee, that sounds great. Yeah, get me one. I'd like to get in on it."

Stacy couldn't gather what they were talking about. But

then she couldn't care less. She had her own problems. Funny, she never felt like that before. Problems were foreign to her.

She was relieved when Giles reached for his coat. "Thanks a lot, Anne," he said, "but we got to get home."

"Yes," Stacy added, "and thanks for letting me go along."

"My pleasure," Anne said, sounding very grown up. "I'm glad you could come."

Again Stacy felt like a little kid.

The other boy and girl bundled into their outer clothing, too. Then they all piled into Anne's car once more, and she drove them home.

Stacy couldn't wait to wave good night at their sidewalk. Now, she thought, as she mounted the front steps, the bombshell would really drop. Almost reluctantly, she unbuttoned her coat and hung it in the hallway. Then, shivering, she went into the living room. Mom and Dad looked towards her.

"Did you have a nice time?" Mom asked.

"Yes. OK." But she didn't want small talk now, not when she was so uptight. She glanced at the fireplace. No warm, pulsing glow showed around the gas log.

"Why don't you start the fire?" she asked.

"We have the furnace heat," Dad told her. "There's no use burning gas just for the looks of it."

Gee, Stacy thought, we can't even have a fire in the fireplace. What gives, anyhow? She stared down at the thick carpeting.

Mom patted her shoulder and pointed to the large, cut-glass bowl. "Here, have some eggnog."

Stacy nodded, faintly aware of the scent of the bayberry candle. She had always loved it.

Grabbing a cup and a handful of cookies, Giles planted himself on a cushion near the tree. "A guy," he began to tell Dad, "—another friend of Anne's—went with us. And he let me in on something good. He's going to give me a letter for five dollars. Then I'll make five copies and—"

Dad was wagging his head. "The old pyramid scheme. Is it resurrected again? Well, just forget about it."

"But you can make a lot of money in no time flat."

Dad wagged his head again. "It's against the law to send such letters through the mail."

"We're not going to mail them," Giles informed him.

"Nevertheless, it's only a get-rich-quick scheme. It's nothing but pure chance that anyone gets anything at all."

Giles didn't seem convinced. "Well, it's only five bucks."

"Only five bucks!" Dad all but shouted. "You talk as though money grew on trees."

Dad's words struck Stacy as strange. He never said anything like that before, and he seldom ever raised his voice. What was wrong with him? Always good-natured, he usually laughed at Giles' money-mad ideas. Now, both he and Mom were acting strange. And on Christmas Eve, too.

Well, she just *had* to ask about the skis before they opened the gifts. She had scanned all the items near the tree, but couldn't see anything as long and narrow as skis. Her heart sank, but she held her breath and plunged in.

"Am I getting my skis, Mom?" Maybe, at least, there'd be a gift certificate for them.

"I'm afraid not." Mom's voice was low but clear.

"But how can I go with Barb next week without them?"

"No problem," Giles offered. "Rent a pair."

Well, that was a way out, she thought, but I wanted my own. She remembered Barb mentioning "light, waxless, super bindings."

Mom was shaking her head. "You couldn't go anyway. I'm sorry."

"But why?" Barb's grandparents lived out there, and they had a huge house. They could easily fit Stacy in, Barb said, so she wouldn't have to pay hotel expenses.

"Well," Mom said, "I'm afraid you're not getting any of the ski outfit, either, and—"

"I have some warm clothes," Stacy cut in. "I could wear them."

"But the fees," Mom continued, "and your airfare, too, wouldn't be exactly cheap."

"But why? What's wrong with—" Stacy began again and stopped. She knew she would cry if she went any farther.

Mom took a deep breath. "Dad's work isn't going to last much longer. The company has been in trouble for some time now."

Dad was the sales director at the Apex Iron Company. He had been for the last ten years—as long as they had been living in this house.

Stacy choked down the full feeling in her throat. "Dad will be out of work?"

"Yes, he'll have to find another position," Mom said.

Giles got up from his cushion and stood looking at Dad, rather amazed. "I heard the guys at school say the plant was laying off, but I didn't know the offices were hit."

Dad ran his hand nervously across his head. "Oh, yes," he said. "I've been on part-time for three weeks. Others have already left for good."

So that was why he was home two days a week, Stacy thought. He often took time off against his vacation to rest or go somewhere, so she never thought anything of it.

Giles spread his hands and hunched his shoulders. "But the guys said someone else is buying the company."

Dad shook his head. "That's what everyone hoped. So far, there's been no luck in that direction. The place is closing at the end of the month."

"You mean there won't be any money coming in to live on?" Giles was blunt.

Putting his hands on the mantel, Dad looked down into the black fireplace. "There will be unemployment insurance for a while. But it will be a lot less than a regular salary." He turned to Stacy and then back to Giles. "I'm sorry about Christmas, but I hoped against hope that the other company would buy in. We just learned this morning that no deal could be made. If it could have, believe me, I'd have gone downtown today and charged everything you both wanted."

Giles gave a little wave of protest. "No problem. Don't worry about that."

But there were worry lines between Mom's brows. "We have to think of the house payments," she said. "Our mortgage is still so high. And we'll have to sell my car. The balance is high on that, too." She sighed. "We'll just have to get along with one car."

"I'll put a notice on Rod's bulletin board," Dad said. Rod's was the garage he always did business with.

"Gee, must you sell it?" Giles asked. He was going to learn to drive soon.

"Yes, we have to cut expenses," Dad told him and waved away any further protest. "We have to be prepared."

Prepared? Stacy thought. How can you prepare for not

living as you always did? O God, why did life have to change so much?

Mom patted her shoulder. "I'm awfully sorry about your skiing trip, but there'll be other years."

"Oh, sure." Stacy couldn't help her bitter feeling. "But why did you say I could go with Barb if you knew I couldn't?"

"I didn't say you could," Mom, always soft-spoken and gentle, defended herself. "You should have waited until—"

Dad turned swiftly. "Don't go blaming your mother. She didn't give you permission."

"Well, I took for granted—"

"Yes, you took for granted," Dad said. He sounded harsh. "You always did. But from now on, don't. You ask permission when you want to do something and when you want to buy something, whether you like it or not."

So that was the way life was going to be. Watch everything you do and say. Well, she *wasn't* going to like it. Just because Dad was losing his job, he didn't have to get mad at her. His stern words filled her with resentment, and she turned away.

There was still another angle to this that she had to consider. "What am I going to tell Barb?" she asked Mom.

"You'll just have to tell her you can't go."

"I can't. She'll get mad."

"Let her get mad," Giles put in bluntly. "Or let her moneybags father stake you to the whole thing." Giles never liked Barb's family. He always said they put on airs.

"No use talking like that, Giles," Dad told him. "They can't help our misfortune. If we can't pay Stacy's way, we don't want her to go."

Stacy again turned to Mom. "I can't tell her. I'd just die."

Mom nodded her understanding. "Well, it's too late tonight, anyway. I'll call her mother tomorrow."

Tomorrow, Christmas Day, Stacy thought, and five hours ago she was so happy about it. Now she wished it would never come. Then she felt the light pressure of Mom's hand on her arm as she led her to the tree.

"We can open the gifts we did get," Mom was saying.

At least two things on Stacy's list were in the packages, the album by Deep Ocean and a purple-plaid skirt. But the skirt wasn't the one in Leckerman's window and not nearly so pretty. Or that was how it seemed to her, anyway. The one in

10

Leckerman's cost forty-nine dollars—she had priced it. That's why she didn't get it. Must everything be measured in dollars from now on? Gee, what a terrible thing to look forward to.

She hoped her face didn't show what she was thinking. Mustering a smile, she said, "Thank you, Mom and Dad. I did want these." And she did, even if the skirt was a different one.

They nodded and smiled over the cologne sets she had given them. And she appreciated the loud "Wow" from Giles when he opened the socket wrenches she gave him. He had spoken enough about them as he planned for the car he'd get when he turned sixteen. But she noted that he received only one of the electronic games he wanted and he didn't get the corduroy sports coat he asked for. He didn't seem to mind, though. But he wasn't giving up a trip he had planned for, as she had to.

They all had some more eggnog before going to bed.

But sleep wouldn't come to Stacy as she tossed and turned. Suddenly she remembered the curlers she was going to put in her hair. But she didn't have the ambition to get up and put them in. To heck with them, let her hair hang straight.

Her disappointment was still keen. But more distressing was the thought of telling Barb about not going with her to Colorado. Even if Mom would call her mother she knew she would have to talk to Barb. Barb had a habit of wanting her own way. Up until now, Stacy never had reason not to let her have it. But tomorrow would be a different story. She didn't have to wonder how Barb would take it—she knew.